TRINITY THINKS TWICE

Trevor Holliday

Barnstork Press

CONTENTS

TREVOR HOLLIDAY

for John M. Holliday and Samuel Holliday V

LUMINARIAS

Sunday night.

One week before Christmas.

In Tucson's Presidio neighborhood, all was calm, all was bright.

Trinity was not interested in breaking his neck.

Balancing himself on a ladder, he pointed the hammer as far as he could reach up the side of his house.

Taking a finishing nail from his mouth, Trinity scratched a line under the fascia.

"High enough?"

Lesley hugged her arms to her sides.

"I can't see," she said. "It's getting too dark."

On the gray planks of the porch lay an ancient roll of multi-colored Christmas lights.

One week before Christmas.

Trinity pulled his tweed jacket close and his dark Stetson low.

Jimmy Stewart in the years between *It's a Wonderful Life* and *Shenandoah*.

Out with the old, he thought.

He would throw the whole tangled string of lights away.

He pounded the nail halfway into the fascia.

"Take a look underneath the lights," he called down to Lesley. "I'll put up the star."

Trinity felt a chill.

Lesley handed him the ornament.

"It's beautiful," she said. "How old is it?"

Trinity stretched his hands above his head and hooked the star to the nail.

"It's at least as old as I am," he said.

Trinity hopped down from the bottom rung of the ladder and plugged in the star.

They walked out to the sidewalk.

He was happy she had taken time from the market to help him decorate.

The reverie was broken by the appearance of Trinity's neighbor.

"Hey Frank, how many of these do you want?"

"Wendell?" Trinity said.

It had gotten too dark to see Wendell Gentry coming down the street.

Just exactly what I need, Trinity thought.

Gray hair pulled back in a ponytail, beetled eyebrows under wire-rimmed glasses, Wendell Gentry pushed a mass of brown paper sandwich bags in front of Trinity.

"You want to put out luminarias?"

Trinity squinted. Wendell and his wife Rosemary hadn't lived in the neighborhood very long.

What was it about Wendell that Trinity found so objectionable?

"I don't know," Trinity said. "What do you have in mind?"

How many bags did Wendell have?

He must have bought out Walgreen's entire supply.

Trinity picked up the old string of lights.

"These can go to the dump," he said to Lesley. "I'll get some more."

"We're trying to get everybody on the street to put these out," Wendell said, pointing his chin at the bags.

Trinity might not like Wendell, but lining the street with luminarias was a good idea. It would lend a festive air.

"Rosemary's busy getting ready for her yard sale," Wendell said. "That's her baby."

Trinity took a couple of the bags.

He looked at Wendell's earnest face, not certain if he should laugh.

Probably not, he decided.

"Sure, I'll put some up."

Lesley turned toward Trinity. "I think it's a great idea."

"I've got some instructions for you," Wendell said. "I'm trying to give an in-service to each person."

Trinity shifted his Tony Lama boots.

An in-service, he thought.

Maybe that's why I don't like him.

Wendell held out a sheet of paper. "It won't take long. It's self-explanatory."

"This is great, Wendell," Trinity said, glancing at the paper, "I mean it."

"Hey, it's an idea," Wendell said. He waved his arm. "All I want to do is help out."

Trinity folded the instructions and tucked them in his jacket. He could probably manage to put together a luminaria.

The instructions would go into the garbage, just like the lights.

"Too late now for me to back out of this, isn't it?" Trinity said.

Night was replacing the dusk.

Trinity noticed a crow near the alley, pecking at garbage near the dumpster.

Wendell vigorously shook his head and grinned, the light from the star revealing a row of uneven teeth beneath his moustache.

"Not a chance, Frank."

Trinity and Lesley watched Wendell leave.

So what if he didn't like Wendell?

Putting out the luminarias was no big task.

Trinity eyed the paper bags.

Open paper bag, he thought.

Fill with sand.

Insert candle.

Light.

"They'll look nice, Frank," Lesley said.

Wendell had brought enough bags to illuminate the street three or four times.

Would he be coming back with candles?

Wendell stood near the end of the street, across

from Jeremy and Margo Powers's antique store.

The store was closed for the evening.

Trinity watched the couple pull their Honda Civic away from the curb.

Wendell would need to act quickly if he wanted to catch them.

"Want to come in?" Trinity said to Lesley.

"I can't tonight," Lesley said. "Six o'clock comes early."

The brake lights on the Civic went on and the car stopped abruptly.

Jeremy jumped out and ran toward the store.

"Somebody must have forgotten something," Trinity said.

Trinity and Lesley stood together beneath the star.

"See you tomorrow?" Trinity asked.

"I'll think about it," she said.

"Great," Trinity said.

He nodded toward the pile of bags and candles and pulled his Zippo lighter from his pocket.

Idly flipped the top and lighted it.

"You know what I'll be doing."

❉   ❉   ❉

"Thanks," Margo Powers said, taking the lunch bags from Wendell. "What a great idea."

Wendell smiled.

"Peace and love," he said.

Margo watched Wendell walk down the street.

Luminarias, she thought.

Well, why not? She tossed the bags in the back seat, rolled up the window of the Civic and waited.

Jeremy's acting stranger than usual, Margo thought.

She glanced at her watch.

Just past six thirty.

At this rate, Margo could count on getting to the gallery sometime before the caterers started putting the leftovers away.

Margo checked her lipstick in the rear view mirror of the Civic.

She looked good. Her long dark hair contrasted favorably with her fair skin and deep green eyes.

Margo and Jeremy weren't invited out every night of the week.

Margo suspected the invitation was sent from the Maxwell Day Gallery by mistake.

The exhibition was a very big event. Three previously unknown works by Maxwell Day were being shown for the first time tonight.

Margo turned the invitation over in her hands.

Margo felt insecure about going to the exhibition.

Maxwell Day's widow was a fixture in the society pages. The local paper's cameras loved Tallie Day.

What would Margo and Tallie have in common?

She chided herself. As if she and Tallie Day would even speak more than three words to each other.

Jeremy, on the other hand...

Jeremy would have no problem making chit-chat.

And he'd find a way to do so.

Jeremy slid into the passenger seat and slammed the door shut.

"Can't forget these," he said, holding out a pair of sunglasses.

Margo shook her head. "We're late," she said.

Jeremy glanced at the invitation.

"I still say it's a form letter."

That angered Margo. What made him such an expert?

They headed north toward the foothills.

Several minutes passed without Margo or Jeremy speaking.

Jeremy broke the silence.

"They must have sent out hundreds of these things."

He picked up the invitation and ran his finger over the ivory stationary.

"You don't think they expect us to go to this thing, do you?"

"Why wouldn't they?" she said. "We're in the same business."

Jeremy laughed. "I thought we were trying to sell antiques."

He shook his head. "Oh excuse me. And estate jewelry."

Margo stared ahead.

Jeremy could be so condescending.

As if their business was a lark.

Holding the invitation up, Jeremy looked at the

watermark.

"Maxwell Day," he said. "How long has he been dead, anyway?"

Jeremy wasn't in bad shape yet, Margo thought. He'd obviously grabbed something to drink when he went back into the shop, but maybe he could manage to get through the evening without making a spectacle of himself.

"Do you want me to turn around?"

She took her foot from the accelerator. "We don't have to go."

Jeremy glared at Margo. "Oh no you don't," he said. "You've gotten me this far."

He threw the invitation onto the dashboard.

"Keep going," he said. "I'm planning to have a good time."

WESTERN ART AND RUMAKI

The Maxwell Day Gallery was decorated for Christmas.

It's beautiful, Margo thought, elegant and festive, just as she would have imagined.

She hesitated in front of the gallery.

Would Jeremy be able to hold things together?

Margo glanced at the invitation. The exhibition would focus on the gallery's collection of Maxwell Day's paintings.

Since Day's death, the painter's work had increased dramatically in value.

Devoted followers of the Tucson artist were almost worshipful in their praise.

Collectors would be eager to see the new paintings.

For good reason, Margo thought.

She peered into the front window of the gallery at the display of perennially popular prints.

Although not particularly enthralled by Western art, Margo had to admit that Maxwell Day's work was magnificent.

Standing under the light in front of the gallery, Jeremy looked like a dissolute British actor in his dark green corduroy jacket.

He bolted into the gallery, not waiting for Margo.

She stood alone in front of the window, wearing her red woolen cape.

She felt like an abandoned schoolgirl.

"Lovely, aren't they?"

Margo turned.

A wave of shock hit her stomach.

Her landlord, Matthew Fenton, stood next to her, looking into the window.

How much rent did they owe Matthew for the shop?

Had they even paid for October?

Margo tried to calm herself. Running was out of the question.

The old man had dressed up tonight.

She had never seen Fenton without his beige windbreaker.

"Matthew, what a surprise," Margo said. "Yes, they are. Absolutely lovely."

She told herself to breathe deeply and relax.

"Each one could tell a story," Fenton said, reaching for Margo. The touch of Fenton's fingers on her arm was cold.

Margo's mind raced, searching for an excuse to make about the rent.

Fenton looked preoccupied.

"I'd love to talk," he said, "maybe we will later."

"That would be great," Margo said. "It's so good to see you."

She exhaled after he walked away.

Thank God that was brief, she thought.

Who would have known Fenton was an art lover?

Margo watched Fenton slide past the front door of the gallery, glancing sideways into the bright interior. Was he looking for someone?

Fenton didn't go in.

✳ ✳ ✳

Margo entered the gentle hubbub of the gallery.

Jeremy had put on his dark glasses. He stood in the bright light next to a chaffing dish, spooning an enormous portion of the hot hors d'oeuvres onto his plate.

Margo felt embarrassed.

She should have known better than to bring Jeremy.

Seeing her reflection in the glass doorway, Margo tried to tell herself that she felt fine.

She picked up a nametag.

MARGO POWERS - PRESIDIO ANTIQUES

It didn't matter what Jeremy did. She would have a good time in spite of her husband.

Margo told herself to mingle. Even if the invitation had been a mistake, she would act as if she belonged there.

A woman smiled at her. "Margo Powers?" the woman said, reading Margo's nametag.

"And you must be Page," Margo answered.

The woman laughed and touched her nametag.

PAGE DAY - THE MAXWELL DAY GALLERY

Margo liked Page immediately.

She was attractive, without looking like she spent hours on herself.

Page spoke to Margo as if they were old friends.

"Presidio Antiques..." Page said. "How fabulous."

"We're just getting started," Margo said, excusing herself immediately for the slight inaccuracy.

"You are?" Page's smile was genuine. "How fabulous. What do you specialize in?"

Margo laughed. "We try to be eclectic. Jeremy likes estate jewelry since he's the one who ends up doing the lifting."

"I need to visit you," Page said.

"Are you ready for Christmas?" Margo asked.

She hoped that her attempt at small-talk didn't seem too artificial.

"I still have last minute shopping to do," Page said. "Can you believe it?"

Margo felt uncomfortable talking about the shop.

Presidio Antiques was on life support.

Fenton wouldn't wait much longer for the rent.

Would it be Margo's luck for Page to visit on the day they were evicted?

"You sell estate jewelry?" Page asked. "That's absolutely too fabulous. Do you appraise things also?"

"Oh sure," Margo said. "That's Jeremy's forte."

She glanced in Jeremy's direction. Jeremy was piling more rumaki onto his plate. Finding no more room, he held one of the skewered water chestnuts in front of his face.

"That's fabulous," Page said. She glanced over her shoulder. "I might need to have some things appraised. Do you have a card?"

"Of course," Margo said. Keeping one eye on Jeremy she fished into her pearl covered clutch. "What do you need to have appraised?"

"Oh, I'll just drop in on you," Page said. She held the card. "Your place sounds fabulous. I really can't wait."

Margo nodded. Seeing someone in the shop besides Jeremy would be a welcome change.

"I'd love that," Margo said. "By the way, this reception is wonderful. Thanks for including us."

"You're more than welcome," Page said. "Actually, you should thank Tallie. She put this together."

Page pointed to a woman holding court near the canapés. Wearing a gorgeous black dress and pearls, Tallie exuded the glamor of a previous era.

Margo froze.

Oh God no, she thought, don't let this happen.

Jeremy lunged around the table.

A plate in one hand, a glass of wine in the other.

He headed directly for Tallie.

Margo closed her eyes, not able to watch what lay ahead.

She opened her eyes. In less than a second, disaster had been averted. None of the rumaki had been spilled. It was still on Jeremy's plate.

The wine was still in his glass.

Miraculous.

Margo watched in amazement as Tallie started to laugh.

Jeremy, as usual, had barely escaped disaster.

He said something to Tallie.

Was Tallie laughing? Margo didn't doubt it. Jeremy could be charming when he put his mind to it.

Tallie put her hand on Jeremy's lapel.

Charming, handsome, witty.

His less endearing qualities were hidden.

Page apparently had missed the near catastrophe.

"I'll definitely come see you," Page said.

"And I'll definitely look forward to that," Margo said. She put her hand on Page's wrist. "Maybe we could have lunch."

"Fabulous," Page said.

* * *

Jeremy couldn't contain his excitement. He slammed the car door shut behind him. "Did you see those paintings?"

Margo started the car and turned the heater up. "No, Jeremy," she said, "I must have missed them."

"Weren't they incredible?" Jeremy said. "Did you see how much they were asking for them?"

Margo glanced at Jeremy. His cheeks were red.

"So," she said, "you're glad that I insisted..."

"You didn't see the prices?"

Margo shook her head. "That's your department, isn't it?"

Of course she had seen the prices.

"Take a guess. How much does one Maxwell Day go for?"

Margo shook her head. "I have no idea. A gazillion, right?"

"Come on," Jeremy said, "take a guess. Take your wildest, most over-the-top guess."

Margo didn't want to play Jeremy's game, but went ahead in an effort to appease him.

"A hundred thousand," she said. She turned her head slightly, expecting a crest-fallen look on Jeremy's face.

She felt mean. He hadn't been this excited in a long time.

"Good guess," he said, unfazed. "That's not far off. Some are that much. But some twice that. Finding one is the real trick. I guess old Max didn't exactly crank them out."

"They're certainly lovely," Margo said.

"Yeah, of course," Jeremy said with a dismissive wave of his hand. "They're great... But can you imagine? A hundred thousand dollars? The guy hasn't even been dead all that long." He slumped into his seat. "Some people would do anything for one of those things."

He's so predictable, Margo thought. The paintings will excite his imagination only for so long.

"A hundred thousand dollars," Jeremy repeated. "Imagine what we could do with that."

God alone knew what Jeremy would do with that kind of money.

Margo knew exactly what she would have to do.

Jeremy looked out the window.

Leaning forward, he pulled out a flask.

Margo felt irritated.

He's as predictable as rain.

"Can't you wait until we get home?"

Jeremy might ignore the question about his drinking.

If not, Margo had just started World War III.

"Give it up Margo," he said.

She didn't answer.

He saluted her with the flask.

"Here's to you," he said. "There's none like you."

Margo shook her head.

Better to simply keep quiet.

"That's a good girl," Jeremy said, putting his hand on her knee.

Wonderful, Margo thought.

Romance.

"What would you do, Margo?"

She glanced at him. "What do you mean?" she said.

Jeremy rolled the window down slightly. "If we had one of those paintings... What would you do with the money?"

Margo shook her head.

She would stop playing his game.

He was asleep before they got home.

With that kind of money, she might travel...

A new car?

She would pay off Fenton.

What would she do if she ever really received that kind of windfall?

Her biggest job would be keeping Jeremy away from it.

She helped him out of the car and left him in the living room, still in his corduroy jacket, sprawled in the recliner.

She turned the lights off in the living room, undressed, got into bed.

Even half asleep she couldn't stop thinking.

FENTON'S CADILLAC

Jeremy climbed, bleary-eyed, out of bed.

Margo was in the kitchen, preparing to leave for the shop.

Monday.

Six days before Christmas.

"I'll be there in a while," Jeremy said.

"Don't be long," she said. "This could be our lucky day."

In light traffic, the store was twenty minutes from the house.

Why couldn't Jeremy just come with her? Keeping two cars was expensive. Traffic was never light.

Our lucky day, Margo thought.

We could sell everything at half price.

Everything.

Even the fixtures.

❋ ❋ ❋

She pulled the Civic up to the curb.

Presidio Antiques.

Margo blew on her hands. Finally, she had become acclimated to Tucson. It took a couple of years, but now she couldn't imagine going through a Cleveland winter again.

Margo touched the lights strung around the doorway of the store. They kept the lights up all year, the little red pepper-shaped lights providing a counterpoint to the purple building.

Matthew Fenton's Cadillac turned the corner.

Margo cringed.

Would this be the showdown? Fenton couldn't possibly carry them any longer.

It might be a relief getting it over with. It was too late to pretend she hadn't seen him.

Margo stood by the front door. The Cadillac slowed down.

This is the end, she thought.

Can't make the rent, can't keep the business.

Just like a game of Monopoly.

She wished Jeremy was here. Jeremy was a good talker. He would think of something to tell Fenton.

Margo pulled a creased pack of cigarettes from her coat pocket and took a tired book of matches from the cellophane.

She tasted the acrid sulfur of the match .

Nothing like the first drag.

Fenton pulled the Cadillac close to the shop. The tires squealed against the curb.

All I need is a handkerchief around my eyes,

Margo thought. I'll be ready for the firing squad.

Fenton took off his sunglasses and put them in his pocket before slowly pulling himself out of the Cadillac.

He doesn't get around well, Margo thought.

I'll stand right here.

I'm not going over to him.

Fenton had gone back to wearing his windbreaker this morning.

He chewed on his usual black cigar.

"How's business?" he said.

He's trying to sound casual, she thought.

How long did he work on the cigars? Margo had never seen him light one.

The cigars were as much a part of Fenton as his bushy eyebrows and the windbreaker.

"Same as it was last week," Margo said. "And the week before that."

"That bad?" Fenton said. He rubbed the point of his chin. "Oh well, things always pick up before Christmas."

Don't listen to him, she thought.

Would it make any difference to Fenton that Christmas was just a few days away?

She didn't know how to read his expression.

Jeremy would know how to handle this, if he were here.

Jeremy would do the talking.

Fenton stood at the front door.

"Come on in," Margo said. "I'll make some coffee."

"Loverly," Fenton said.

Why am I doing this? Margo wondered.

* * *

Fenton rubbed the palm of his hand across the top of the coffee cup. His eyes followed Margo.

She moved around the store, snapping on lights in the display cases, getting the place ready for business.

"Coffee will be ready soon," she said.

Where was Jeremy?

Margo felt anxious.

Jeremy never took this long.

"Did I ever tell you how I got started in business?"

The question surprised Margo.

"You have not," Margo said. She stood in front of Fenton, her hand on the curve of her hip.

He keeps looking at me, Margo thought.

Where the hell is Jeremy?

"I started in the same business as you," Fenton said, "out on the East Side."

"I didn't know that," Margo said. "Furniture? Jewelry?"

"All that," Fenton said. "Objets d'art, mostly."

He pronounced the word with a care that surprised Margo.

The coffee was ready.

Margo poured some for Fenton.

Jeremy was never this late.

"I hardly step foot in the place any more." Fenton shrugged "I have to take care of my other ventures."

Like collecting rent, she thought.

Could she change the subject?

Stall?

"How did you happen to be at the gallery last night?"

Fenton lifted his watery blue eyes.

"Max was an old friend of mine."

"You knew Maxwell Day?"

Fenton laughed.

"You bet. Max and I were inseparable."

❋ ❋ ❋

Fenton didn't mention the rent.

"Max was a financial disaster." Fenton held his cigar loosely. "I had to bail him out... I don't know how many times."

Fenton continued following Margo with his eyes as she moved around the room.

"I'd lend him money, but I always got something in return."

Margo's breathing became shallow.

"Well, that's good," she said.

Fenton smiled.

"I got a few of his paintings that way."

He held the palm of his hand toward Margo.

"Hey, just a couple. And I was taking a gamble."

Margo shook her head.

"That's amazing."

Fenton grimaced.

"Not really. I was his friend. How much do you suppose they're worth now?"

The string of sleigh bells on the front door rang. Jeremy was here.

Margo felt relieved.

Jeremy hung up his jacket, grabbed a cup and poured some coffee.

"Good morning Matthew," he said.

Margo gave Jeremy a peck on the cheek.

"He hasn't said anything about the rent," she whispered.

Fenton sipped his coffee.

"Maybe you might know," he said to Jeremy. "I was just asking your wife how much she thought Max Day's paintings were worth... If I wanted to sell one."

As if he wouldn't know, Margo thought.

"You're right on time, Jeremy," she said.

"They're probably worth a fortune," Margo said.

"What are we talking about?" Jeremy asked. "You've got one of his paintings?"

Fenton nodded. "A couple," he said. "I was telling Margo about them."

Jeremy's eye's widened. "Unbelievable," he said. "Any way I can see them?"

Fenton turned from Jeremy back to Margo.

"It's funny," Fenton said, "I was thinking about this last night. You look a little like Tallie."

"Of course," he added, "when Tallie was

younger."

"I take that as a complement," Margo said.

Fenton nodded. "You should. She was a knock-out. You should have seen her forty years ago." He whistled through his teeth. "Needless to say," he added, "I was no slouch either, back then."

"I'm sure that you weren't," Margo said.

"Max was a fool… She was in a league of her own."

The old man's eyes were almost shut.

Abruptly, Fenton came out of his reverie.

He started to stand.

Getting to his feet took a huge effort.

Unlighted cigar still clenched between his teeth. "I gotta go," he said.

"We'll walk you out," Margo said, picking Fenton's windbreaker up from the back of his chair. "Won't we Jeremy?"

Fenton put his windbreaker on.

"That's all right," he said. "I know where my car is."

Jeremy slapped the old man on the back. "Hey, I'd love to see those paintings."

Not one word, Margo thought.

Not one single word about the rent.

Maybe she had misjudged Matthew Fenton.

She handed him the windbreaker.

"I'm sorry we haven't paid you," Margo said.

The words simply came out.

She hadn't planned to say anything about the rent.

Jeremy gave her a look.

She didn't care.

Fenton stopped.

He looked at Margo and nodded.

He clenched the black cigar in his teeth and blinked his eyes.

"I understand," he said. "We'll work something out."

Fenton turned to Jeremy. "You got some time? I'll show those paintings to you right now. Follow me in your car."

Jeremy looked at Margo. "Can you spare me?"

She nodded. "I think I can handle things."

Jeremy brushed Margo's cheek with his lips.

"You were right," he whispered. "This might be our lucky day."

THREADBARE COUCH AND PAINTED COYOTE

Christmas carols rattled on a tape deck in the reception area of Joe Sawyer's law office, a run-down adobe at the end of Meyer Avenue.

So who really gave a damn about Christmas?

Ed Carney sure didn't. All the tinsel and ornaments in the world couldn't budge him from his Scrooge-like attitude.

This was Sawyer's idea of service?

The receptionist smiled at Ed.

Careful, baby, Ed thought.

I'm bad news.

"Joe's almost ready for you," she said. "He had to take this call.

Just paying for the consult was bad enough.

It would be hell scraping together the dough to

retain Sawyer.

Despite the shabby office, Ed knew Sawyer didn't come cheap.

He could get anyone a good deal.

In a way, that pissed Ed off.

Most of the people Sawyer represented *needed* to serve time.

Ed's case was different. He knew a setup when he saw one.

He glanced at the girl.

Nothing special there, he thought.

Acting busy, as if she was typing something up for Mr. F. Lee Sawyer back there.

A *huge* setup.

How could he have known that Tina Harlow had on a wire?

He wouldn't have suspected Tina.

Not in a million years.

Tina had done well on probation and she was almost at the end of it.

She wasn't a hardened criminal by any stretch of the imagination.

She had a classy look with her blonde hair and a figure to match.

So what if Tina had kited a couple of checks from her boss's account?

So what?

Who didn't?

He glanced at Sawyer's receptionist again.

Well, probably not her...

But Tina's boss probably had it coming.

Lousy bastard was probably putting the moves on her every chance he could get.

Ed should have known something was up by the way that Tina pushed him away.

She'd never done that any of the other times.

Neither had any of the others.

The investigation was a witch-hunt and Ed was the target.

He would never get used to the way the department had changed in the last few years.

* * *

Sawyer was taking forever.

Ed flipped through the year-old magazine collection and looked around the office.

The receptionist was still typing.

A painting of a coyote hung above a threadbare couch.

What the hell did Sawyer do with his money?

He sure didn't spend it on décor.

LUCKY DAY

Jeremy and Fenton were gone.

Alone in the shop, Margo wondered whether she should even bother keeping the place open.

No, she thought.

She clenched her hands so tightly her nails dug into her palms.

Trying to push away the terrible thought.

No... Jeremy wouldn't do that.

Margo shook her head.

He wouldn't do it.

Jeremy wouldn't steal a painting.

Margo knew him as well as she knew herself.

Sure, he had his quirks...

Who didn't?

Our lucky day.

She was the one with *that* bright idea.

"Don't do it, Jeremy," she said.

She sat down at the table and put her head in her hands.

She knew him.

He wouldn't steal a painting.

At least she hoped he wouldn't.

THE WORST CASE SCENARIO

"You understand, Ed," Joe Sawyer said, leaning back in his chair, "in today's climate, this kind of case is stacked against you."

Sawyer sniffed.

Ed noticed the lawyer's red eyes.

If he were on my case load, Ed thought, I'd make him do a piss-test every week.

Random intervals.

Sawyer sure as hell didn't waste money on furniture.

The chair Ed sat in was not comfortable.

It reminded him of the replica electric chair where he'd once been seated in a Nogales bar.

Ed had a pretty good idea where Sawyer's money went.

"And with the taped evidence," Sawyer held up the palms of his hands in a gesture of futility. "We'll try for the best deal we can…"

Ed felt blood rushing to his head.

He was going to explode.

The fake electric chair in Nogie had been wired up to a car battery and was designed to give a mild charge to test the machismo of patrons.

Ed's current sensation was created by his nerves alone.

"What the hell do you mean *we*?" Ed said.

Sawyer wrinkled his eyes and forehead.

"Relax, Ed. It's a figure of speech."

"Yeah," Ed said, "I'm familiar with the general concept."

He leaned forward in the uncomfortable chair.

Ed's mother would describe the chair's style as Spanish Mission.

Gladys never hesitated to pour perfume on any pig.

Ed tried to focus his attention back on Sawyer.

The consult was going badly, and he blamed the lawyer.

"I'm sorry, Joe. I'm a little on edge here. Why don't you do us both a favor and cut the crap?"

Something between a smile and a smirk flickered across Sawyer's deadpan face.

"How long have you *been* a probation officer, Ed?"

Ed leaned back in the wooden chair and did some mental calculations. "Seventeen years in April. Why?"

"You know the drill then, right?"

Sawyer was a cat playing with a dead canary.

He sniffed again.

"I should," Ed said.

The condescending bastard was a cokehead.

Ed was sure of it.

Sawyer nodded and screwed his fingers together on top of his desk.

"So get over it. You took your chances. You got caught."

Unscrewed his fingers and started drumming on his desk.

"I'll get you the best deal I can," Sawyer said, "but it's going to take some money."

Now who's a predator? Ed thought.

He glanced at Sawyer's diplomas.

Ed and Sawyer were about the same age.

It was depressing.

Seventeen years in probation and Ed hadn't saved a dime.

Whereas this guy was living on easy street.

"What's the bottom line?" Ed asked.

Sawyer grinned, showing a line of straight, white teeth.

Caps, Ed thought.

"Bottom line?" Sawyer sniffed again. "Get me twenty-five hundred and I'll enter a notice of appearance. You have a clean record, which is nice. You're already on disciplinary leave, so the judge might not want to slam you too hard."

Sawyer dabbed at his nose.

All the money he doesn't spend on decor goes up his nose, Ed thought.

Sawyer sniffed again.

Ed would have liked a chance to rearrange

Sawyer's face.

Nose first.

"Worst case scenario? A couple of years... Suspended, in all likelihood. You'll have to comply with normal terms of probation. Like I said, you know the drill..."

You bet I know the drill, Ed thought, pushing his way out of the seat.

"Get some letters," Sawyer said as Ed turned toward the door. "Spend some time with your family. It's Christmas."

Letters? Was Sawyer nuts? Would any judge in Pima County give a damn what kind of Boy Scout Ed Carney was?

And family?

Ed's mother?

That was another joke.

"You take plastic?" Ed said.

Sawyer shook his head. "Sorry Charley... Just cash."

❋ ❋ ❋

Leaving Sawyer's office, Ed stood in front of the receptionists desk. A full box of tissues stood on the corner.

Cash.

Ed's spirits had taken yet another nosedive hearing that.

"Your boss could use those tissues," he said.

She shook her head quickly, barely looking up

from her Selectric.

Ed's mother lived a few blocks from Sawyer's office. Gladys had lived in the Presidio for years, surrounded by misfits.

Did she still forget to collect the rent from her tenants?

Ed shook his head.

What was the point of being a slumlord if you didn't make it pay?

Gladys could give him the cash.

Ed hated the idea, but what other options did he have?

He pounded his fists together. They had him where they wanted him.

Screwed and tattooed.

The department set him up, all right. Got Tina to encourage him, got her to lead him on.

Ed should have seen it coming.

When he saw the transcript of the tape, he knew that he didn't stand a snowball's chance.

The receptionist looked up as Ed left.

"Merry Christmas ahead of time," she said.

Ed didn't answer.

AN UNINTERRUPTED JOY RIDE

Page Day turned off the shower.

She took a towel from the rack and stood in front of the mirror.

On a day like this, she might as well be drinking.

I'm drifting away again, she thought.

Walker's no help.

Everything's easy for him.

His whole life is one long, uninterrupted joy-ride.

Walker would be at the gallery right now.

Page pictured him walking on the dark tiled floor of the gallery.

Impeccable in his blue blazer and shined boots, he would be chatting up visitors with anecdotes about his famous father.

Why wouldn't Tallie let her work at the gallery?

Page looked at herself in the mirror.

The reception had gone well. She could mingle

as well as anyone.

Nothing had gone wrong. She hadn't even been tempted by the wine.

Not even for a second.

Page's faults were apparent only to Tallie.

It wasn't about her drinking.

Page hadn't had a drink in a year.

In over a year, to be exact.

She didn't miss it at all.

It wasn't fair, Page thought.

Page had gone to treatment just like a good girl.

Dr. Healey had given her the green light to come home with no hesitation.

Treatment, she thought.

The center had been billed as "A calm and comfortable place to recover."

Maybe she should have just stayed there.

What could she do now?

It wasn't fair being treated like this.

Page knew why she couldn't work at the gallery.

She put her foot on the vanity and worked the towel along her leg.

Tallie called the shots.

She would never let Page work at the Maxwell Day Gallery.

Walker wouldn't have anything to say about it until Tallie died.

It didn't take much insight to understand Tallie's reasoning.

If Page came to the gallery, what would Tallie's role be?

The gallery belonged to Tallie.

Tallie wouldn't give up her stake in the place.

Tallie would never want a younger Mrs. Day working in the gallery.

It was Tallie who had decided Page had a drinking problem, and so Page had gone off to treatment.

Would it always be like this?

Probably, she thought.

At least until Tallie's gone.

The phone rang. Page considered letting the answering machine take care of it. She hated standing naked, talking on the phone.

It probably was a solicitor, anyway. They were always calling at the most inopportune times.

On the other hand, she thought, it could be Walker.

Better to pick it up.

It was Tallie.

"You and Walker are still on for dinner tomorrow night, aren't you?"

Damn, Page thought.

The dinner.

A command performance.

She had forgotten all about it.

"Of course," Page said. "What can I bring?"

Tallie never allowed Page to bring anything.

"Just yourselves, dear," Tallie paused. "I have something very important to discuss with you."

"We'll be there," Page said.

"It's very important," Tallie said.

THE DRAGON

Alice Cooper's *No More Mr. Nice Guy* blared from the jukebox while Ed lined up his shot. A routine bank to drop the eight. After his meeting with Joe Sawyer, Ed stopped at the Dragon. He needed to think things over. It was still early, and the place would be deserted until the lunch crowd arrived. In the meantime, Ed had the place to himself.

A place to relax and think things through.

No way could he miss the shot. He cradled the cue in the slot of his fingers, pulled the stick back…

"Eddie…"

Ed flinched. The cue ball skittered down the table, missing the eight ball entirely before dropping into the corner pocket.

"Eddie-boy, did I make you scratch?"

Ed had never liked Roy Burns.

Ed hated knowing that as long as he lived in Tucson, he would keep running into guys from the department.

From now on, Ed decided, the Dragon was off his list of haunts.

Roy put both hands on the table while Ed took another half-hearted shot at the eight.

"Game?" Roy asked.

Ed shrugged. The last thing he wanted to do was discuss things with Roy, but he'd just bought a pitcher of beer.

Waste not, want not.

That was one of Ed's sayings.

Ed took a drag on a cigarette and placed it on the edge of the pool table.

"Might as well," he said.

He took the cue and scraped the remaining balls into pockets.

Roy fished a couple of quarters from his pocket. The balls clattered under the table.

Ed put the balls in the rack and pointed the cue at Roy.

"You want to break?"

"Seriously," Roy said, "what are you going to do? You got any plans at all?"

Ed sighed as Roy gave a weak effort on the break.

"Yeah," he said, "I'm joining the foreign legion."

Ed knew his options were limited. For seventeen years he'd been a probation officer. Even if Joe Sawyer could work magic, Ed still would need a job.

He could forget law-enforcement.

What the hell else could he do?

"Any ideas?" Ed said.

"Bouncer?" Roy said.

The corners of Ed's mouth turned down.

"You should go into career counseling, Roy, you got a real knack."

"Just trying to be helpful," Roy said.

"One thing I want to know," Ed said, "What's happening with the girl?"

"Like what?" Roy said.

He said it a little too fast. Making too much of an effort at nonchalance. Ed had hit a nerve.

"You know what I mean."

Roy looked uncomfortable.

Ed picked up his beer. "Who's she going to set up next? She got a full time job, or what?"

Roy missed the shot, an easy one.

He whacked the pool cue against the side of the table.

"You'll be lucky not to get jail time," he said. "You should've kept it zipped."

He pulled a cigarette from his shirt pocket.

Ed held up his hands and backed away from the table.

"Don't worry, pal. I won't be coming back here. I just watched seventeen years go down the shitter."

Roy could put on a good show, but everybody knew that Ed would get the sack.

All this phony friendship was bullshit on Roy's part. The son-of-a-bitch was sticking the needle in.

They both knew it.

Ed drank the beer.

Slamming the mug down, he looked directly at Roy. "You can cut the shit, Burns."

Roy stared at Ed. "You made us all look bad.

Ed felt the sting of Roy's words.

He threw his stick on the table, sending solids

and stripes in all directions.

"I gotta go," he said.

Roy shook his head and lit his cigarette. "Suit yourself."

Ed stumbled toward the door feeling anger well up.

Why did he come here, anyway? Who did he expect to see?

"Hey Ed…"

He knew he should have gotten out of the bar quicker.

Don't turn, he told himself. Keep walking.

He turned.

Roy tossed one of the stripes up and down in his hand.

"Don't try and get back at Tina."

Ed felt cold hatred for Roy.

Don't try to get back at Tina.

How the hell did Roy even know Tina's name?

How close were they?

"I mean it, Ed," Roy said. He rolled the ball back onto the table in the direction of the side pocket. "You're not on the team anymore."

The winter sun blazed brightly in the midday sky, temporarily blinding Ed as he left the Dragon.

He pulled the keys to his Trans-Am out of his pocket, still furious.

He had to get control of himself.

It didn't matter what Roy said. Ed had bigger fish to fry.

Twenty-five hundred dollars worth.

MIND OVER MATTER

Visiting Gladys depressed Ed.

Ed didn't understand his mother's choice of neighborhoods.

She could live anywhere in Tucson, but Gladys chose this barrio.

Nothing but crumbling dives populated by old hippies.

Whenever Ed gave Gladys his opinion, she treated him to one of her that-shows-how-much-you-know looks.

Ed preferred the part of Tucson where he himself lived.

The Casa Solana Apartments were almost brand new.

Even in the middle of winter lots of women sunbathed by the pool.

Ed's neighbor Eileen was out there every day.

Va-va-va-voom.

Unfortunately, Eileen also had a boyfriend who looked like a mean son-of-a-bitch.

As if Ed didn't have enough to worry about.

Driving north on Oracle, Ed reviewed his situation. He needed to think things over.

So he'd been set up.

That was obvious.

So what?

Wouldn't I just love to pay somebody back? Ed thought.

He slapped the top of the steering wheel.

There was no point in going down that road.

He would lose.

How many slobs violated their probation trying for revenge?

Even if he got any satisfaction, it would be temporary.

Eventually it would come back to haunt him.

So much for that, Ed thought.

Roy Burns was just like the rest of the sons-of-bitches in the department.

Hypocrites. Not one of them would have done anything differently.

As of this moment, he didn't have any friends, and what was more, he didn't need any.

Ed squinted into the noonday sun.

I should go see Gladys, he thought.

Get it over with.

He shook his head.

The time wasn't right.

He needed a strategy.

It wasn't Christmas yet. His mother would get him to perform some dumb task, like holding the end of a string of lights while she punched staples into the walls of her ancient adobe house.

Worse than that, she might pull out some of the old family photo albums.

No thanks, Ed thought.

No thanks with cheese on top.

He needed to collect himself.

Put together a plan.

He was down, but he sure as hell wasn't out.

He would go home and slap a steak on the grill, grab a beer, kick back.

The answer would come to him.

It was just a case of mind over matter.

Drill Sergeant Barrett in basic training liked using that expression in the middle of PT.

"It's mind over matter, gentlemen," Barrett always said. "I don't mind, and it don't matter."

Yeah, Ed thought.

I don't mind and it don't matter.

He needed a plan.

He also needed twenty-five hundred bucks.

Gladys was his best hope.

Short of larceny, maybe his only hope.

There was an inflated gorilla on the roof of a tire store on Oracle.

Ed used the parking lot to turn the Trans-Am around.

Headed back downtown.

Might as well be a good son.

What the hell.

It's Christmas.

THE GOLD TRANS-AM

Pull yourself together, Margo told herself.

There's no reason this afternoon will be any different from all of last week.

Fenton might give them a break, but the store was still dead.

Who wants estate jewelry?

Nobody.

Not at Christmas.

The newspaper reported that people were spending money like crazy.

At the malls, she thought.

Margo felt sick.

She had overreacted to what Jeremy said.

According to Jeremy she did it all the time.

So Jeremy was going to look at Fenton's paintings.

What was she thinking?

Did she think Jeremy was planning to steal them?

He wouldn't do that.

Jeremy wouldn't do anything like that.

All she was doing was torturing herself.

She needed to get busy here in the store.

Busy doing what?

The emptiness of the store felt eerie. Margo rattled around in it, inventing things to do, rearranging displays.

She needed a smoke.

Standing in front of the shop, Margo pulled out her second cigarette of the day.

She looked at it.

Pathetic.

She even had to ration her cigarettes.

❊ ❊ ❊

Their shop was too far from 4th Avenue, too far from the University, too far from anywhere.

Who came here to shop?

What was the name of that woman at the gallery?

Page.

Page said she'd heard about the shop.

Good things.

She was just being nice.

What was the word she kept saying?

Margo took a drag and let the smoke slowly drift away.

Fabulous…

Margo laughed.

Page must have said the word fabulous a hundred times.

The Presidio Market looked busy.

They don't have trouble getting business, Margo thought.

A man came out of the Presidio Market putting a lid on a Styrofoam cup of coffee.

He got into a gold Trans-Am.

A seventies car, Margo thought.

She lifted her shoulders.

They do more business because they sell coffee.

She stretched.

Strange, Margo thought. The man in the Trans-Am drove the car to the other end of the street and stopped.

Why didn't he just walk?

She shook her head.

Why on earth was she thinking this way?

Why not just grit her teeth and get through the holiday season?

Anything could happen in the New Year.

The paint on the frame of the store's front window was chipping.

She should get Jeremy to fix it.

Spruce the place up. Make it more inviting. She took her finger and ran it along the wood, feeling the loose paint furl under her nail.

Maybe Jeremy could paint the whole shop.

Why stop with the window frames? Why not change the color?

Was purple a mistake?

She could almost start to feel optimistic. Fenton had been reasonable.

Maybe she had misjudged him.

She looked at the store. Trying to be objective. The purple looked dingy.

Purple was a mistake.

Fenton was going to give them a break. She tried to let the information sink in.

She hoped Jeremy would use his head.

Jeremy was the problem.

She felt like she was walking on a tightrope.

Who could say what Jeremy would do next?

Jeremy was fun when they first got together.

Margo remembered the little apartment in Cleveland they had fixed up. That first Christmas they even went caroling together.

Jeremy insisted on the move to Arizona. The shop in Cleveland had done well. Jeremy and Margo put away a little money.

Enough to get this one started, she thought.

Enough to get it started and see it fail.

She shook her head.

Why did she keep thinking so negatively?

They had a few things going for them.

Jeremy had a knack for buying and selling. He could spot items of value at a glance, and he never overpaid for them. He said he spent a previous life as a jewelry trader in a Damascus bazaar.

Just one of Jeremy's stories. You couldn't tell if he was serious or joking.

She looked at the peeling paint.

The store needed attention.

Jeremy would take care of it.

It's beginning to look a lot like Christmas, Margo thought.

A man in whiteface, wearing a dark blue velvet jacket over a red and white striped jersey turned the corner. He staggered under the weight of a wooden box he held on his shoulder.

He stopped in front of Margo and put the box down at her feet. Using his hands, he gestured toward the box, and then toward the window.

Margo watched the man's silent performance.

The man's face was angelic.

He pointed between the wooden box and the store window, pantomiming paintbrush strokes.

"You want to paint the window," Margo said.

The man arched his eyebrow and nodded.

Stepping away from the window, he started a new performance.

Holding his hands on his waist, the man's face contorted in a silent roar of laughter.

His body shook.

Tears of joy came from his eyes.

The performance astounded Margo.

"Wonderful," Margo muttered, "Santa Claus."

The man stopped laughing and stood in front of Margo, a delighted grin crossing his face.

He held his forefinger to his nose.

Right-on-the-money.

He pointed at the box, and then at the window, rolling his shoulders forward in a gesture of inquiry.

"Sorry, pal," Margo said. "No budget for that."

The man shrugged, meeting Margo's words with equanimity.

Slowly, he picked up the wooden box, giving Margo a sweeping bow from his waist.

"Oh, what the hell," Margo said. She held up her finger.

"Wait," she said.

The man in the velvet jacket waited, while Margo went into the store.

Rummaging through her purse, she found a five dollar bill.

Why am I doing this, she wondered.

She knew why.

She wanted to.

Almost Christmas.

The man in the velvet jacket held the bill in front of himself. His eyes wide open with shocked delight.

Carefully, he folded the bill once, twice, and a third time before wedging it into the hinged top of the wooden box.

Margo clapped.

She might not be able to spare the money, but she couldn't have sent the man away empty-handed.

He pointed at the window again.

"I can't do it," Margo said. "I'd love to, but maybe next year."

Struggling under the weight, the man hoisted

the box onto his shoulder, tipped his head once more to Margo, and made his way down the street.

Margo tossed the cigarette onto the sidewalk and ground it out with the pointed toe of her red high heeled shoe.

That's our pedestrian traffic, she thought, following the man's progress as he disappeared around the corner.

Margo turned back to the store. She heard the phone ring.

She let it ring for a while before answering.

Jeremy sounded excited.

"What took you so long?" he asked.

"Where are you?" Margo said.

"I'm still at Fenton's."

She looked at her watch. How long had he been gone?

She felt her skin chill.

"Did he show you the paintings?"

"You wouldn't believe it," Jeremy said. "Hey, he's coming. I gotta go."

Margo closed her eyes.

"We've got it made, baby," Margo heard him say before the receiver clicked.

No, she thought.

No, no, no.

BREAKFAST OF
A CHAMPION

Gladys put the bowl of corn flakes in front of Ed.

She was still in her bathrobe and this was her idea of brunch.

After a lifetime of experience, Ed was used to his mother's habits.

No sugar, no eggs, no orange juice.

Powdered milk.

Good thing he brought his own coffee.

Gladys frowned at the paper cup Ed brought from the Presidio Market.

"How much did that cost?" she asked.

This wasn't going well, Ed thought. He needed the money, but Gladys wouldn't make it easy.

"I gotta have my coffee."

Gladys shook her head. "If you only knew what it does to your nervous system."

Ed laughed.

"You know me, Ma. I never been nervous in my life."

He tried for a Cagney inflection, but as always, it

was lost on his mother.

"Not yet," Gladys said ominously.

"So," Ed said, "You still got the guest house rented?"

"Oh yes," Gladys said. "And he's very quiet. Not a bit of trouble. You remember him, Ed. He's very quiet going in and out. He's a night owl."

Ed remembered him.

A classic deadbeat. Noel had smirked when Gladys had introduced him to Ed.

"So is he paying rent?" Ed asked.

Gladys dipped a tea bag slowly into her cup of warm water.

Ed watched her pull the bag out of the cup.

She put the bag in a saucer.

"He's fallen on some hard times, Ed. He'll pay when he can."

That meant he was not paying rent.

Ed knew how to interpret his mother's words.

"His name is Noel," Gladys said. "Noel Brisbane... Isn't that fascinating?"

Ed pushed the corn flakes around in his bowl.

"I've never heard a name quite like that," Gladys said. "Have you?"

This would be the time to ask for the money, Ed thought.

Not that Gladys didn't have plenty of money to spare.

"You never come down here," Gladys said. "How's work?"

"It's still there," Ed said.

"The girls still won't leave you alone?"

Ed looked up sharply.

What did his mother mean by that?

She couldn't know...

Ed relaxed.

Gladys's expression was pleasant.

How would she know about the mess at work?

He watched Gladys drop the tea bag into the cup and quickly pull it back out.

She wouldn't know.

How much did this Brisbane owe Gladys, anyway? Ed took a gulp of his coffee.

Maybe he could go into the collection business.

"How much does he owe you, Ma?" Ed asked.

Gladys stood up.

Picked up her cup and saucer.

"Heavens, Ed. I don't know. Two or three months, I suppose. Take a look at the receipt book. It's right where it always is."

Ed took another slug of the coffee.

Cold.

Gladys was right. Ed knew where she kept the receipts.

This might work out, he thought.

* * *

Ed was a pro at night surveillance.

He watched Noel get into his battered Volvo and start off on one of his mystery jaunts.

Noel sure as hell wasn't heading to a job.

Ed moved his frame around.

Trying to get comfortable, he rotated his head and neck in a circle.

Every instinct in Ed's body told him Noel was up to no good.

The third key on the ring worked. Ed slid it in with a minimum of effort. Good thing he'd grabbed a can of three-in-one oil along with the keys.

The receipts were revealing.

Noel hadn't paid rent since the early summer.

Some deal the little puke had going, Ed thought.

The corners of Ed's mouth turned down.

It was turning out to be a blessing.

Ed was taking care of his mother's interests.

Who else would?

Sure as hell not Noel Brisbane.

Noel would rip her off in a second.

Ed had seen it happen a thousand times.

He hadn't liked Noel from the start.

The smirk said it all.

Out of habit, Ed held a handkerchief around his hand as he pushed open the door to the small guest house.

Including late fees Ed would assess, Noel's rent would pay Sawyer's retainer.

The cash would amount to a short term loan from Gladys to Ed. And she would never have to know about it.

The wooden plank floor of Noel's house creaked under Ed's weight.

He bumped his shin into the leg of a chair placed about a foot from the door.

Ed hissed through clenched teeth.

The walls were like Gladys's, Ed thought, about two feet thick. Even in daylight hours, no sunlight could creep in.

Noel keeps his crib crowded, Ed thought.

Pulling out his flashlight, Ed snapped the beam onto a utility table, covered by a sheet.

Ed trained the light on the table.

What's under the sheet?

Ed scanned the remainder of the room.

Would Noel be weird enough to have a corpse in here?

Two easels were set up in the room, along with a couple of half finished paintings.

Great, Ed thought. Starving artists make great renters.

Noel might really be up to something twisted.

Ed pulled the sheet from the table, exposing a glass jewelry case.

So that's it. The little creep is a cat burglar.

Ed cracked the lid of the case open, and picked up a long diamond necklace.

What the hell was Noel doing with this stuff?

It has to be hot. No other explanation for it.

From outside, Ed heard Noel's Volvo pulling in.

Ed recognized the sound.

No other car sounds like a Volvo.

He'd learned everything he knew from years on the job, much of this knowledge contained in syllogistic form:

Only assholes drive Volvos.

Noel drives a Volvo.

Therefore, Noel is an asshole.

* * *

Ed heard Noel pull his emergency brake.

He would have less than a minute to get out of the place.

This wasn't the time to go face to face with Noel.

He would come back later for that.

Sometime tonight.

Ed dropped the necklace, snapped the jewelry case shut and pulled the dusty sheet back over the top. No time to look at all the loot, but Ed was willing to bet there was more where it came from.

He pointed the beam of the flashlight toward the kitchen at the same time he heard Noel put his key in the front door.

DISTRIBUTING THE VOTIVES

Wendell held out the votive candles to Trinity.

"Take as many as you need," he said. "We got plenty."

"How's the project going?" Trinity asked.

"It's going well," Wendell said. "I still haven't gotten the old gentleman across the street to come to the door."

"Tom?" Trinity said. "He probably just didn't hear you. Leave me a few extra and I'll make sure he gets them."

Wendell shook his head. "I'd feel better if I did it."

"That's fine," Trinity said.

"Don't worry about it at all," Wendell said. "I'll get the bags and the candles to him."

"Better do it soon," Trinity said. "He might be gone for a couple of days."

He barely noticed Wendell leave.

❋ ❋ ❋

Wendell knocked on Tom's door.

Would anyone appreciate his efforts?

At least they would like the results.

Tom was the last person on the street.

Wendell knocked again.

Tom really was an old man. Would he even bother putting out the luminarias?

There was no answer.

Wendell knocked more loudly.

EGG DROP SOUP

Usually, unlocking his own front door gave Noel more trouble.

Most of the time it stuck just a little, requiring Noel to apply just the right pressure to the top of the door handle.

This time the key worked perfectly.

Noel snapped on the lights.

Merry Christmas.

How many more days was it until Christmas?

He needed to get some rent to take to Gladys.

Noel opened the cupboard over the sink and took out a pack of noodles.

Noel turned on the radio.

He liked classical music with dinner.

Would tonight be productive?

Would it even be worth going out?

The water started to boil. Noel opened the noodles.

Protein, Noel thought. He took the last egg from the refrigerator, cracked it on the side of the pan, and stirred it into the noodles.

How could he be this late with the rent?

He should have gone to Fenton earlier.

Going to Fenton now would be like begging, and Fenton would sense that.

And Fenton could make things difficult if he sensed desparation.

How long would it take before Gladys decided to evict him?

He hated going to Fenton for a handout.

If Fenton had a job for him, though…

Noel stirred the noodles, watching the egg whites swim in the broth.

Fenton and Gladys… I'm dependent on both of them.

Maybe Fenton would have a job for him.

In general, Noel liked working for Fenton.

Fenton's jobs gave him a chance to use his talents.

BULLDOZER

Wendell knocked on Tom's door again. It was already dark. Tom had to be here. Wendell saw the battered jalopy in front of the house.

The door opened. There was very little light in the house, but Wendell saw a smile cross Tom's wrinkled face. "I know you," he said. "You live down the street, right?"

Wendell nodded and grinned.

"That's me," he said. "My wife and I just moved here."

"I hope you like it," Tom said.

"We do," Wendell said. "Of course, we did our homework before moving here. Most people just want to build a cocoon when they retire." Wendell made a face and gestured with his hands. "You know... golf, tennis, arts and crafts."

"I like golf," Tom said. "I haven't played much lately though."

Wendell was a bulldozer.

"Rosemary and I want to help people."

"That's admirable," Tom said. "What can I do for you?"

Wendell showed Tom the bags.

"You want me to put out a couple of luminarias?"

"Exactly." Wendell said. "And I have guidelines that I can go over with you, if you have a moment."

"Come on in," Tom said. "I got a moment."

✻ ✻ ✻

"So," Wendell said, "how long have you lived here?"

Tom raised his eyebrows. "I moved back just a couple of years ago, but I was born right here."

Wendell raised his eyebrows.

"Born in the back room," Tom said. "Right here in this house."

"Fascinating," Wendell said.

He wasn't looking at Tom.

Wendell wondered if Tom realized what he had, hanging on the white plaster wall of his living room. It was dark, but Wendell could see it. He couldn't believe his eyes. A Maxwell Day.

Tom pointed to the back of the house.

"That part, my father added after my sister was born. I'd show you, but it's a mess."

Wendell didn't care about the rest of the house. He couldn't take his eyes from the painting.

Tom noticed Wendell staring at the painting.

"You like that?" he asked. "A friend of mine did it."

Wendell couldn't believe it.

The painting would be worth a fortune.

MISS MUFFET

Noel Brisbane walked toward his beat-up Volvo.

The Volvo was the quintessential Tucson car.

No rust, very few dents.

There were probably several hundred cars just like it in Tucson.

A legion of beige four-doors, baking under the desert sun.

The desert night sky was pitch black. A mesquite branch caught Noel's shirt and ripped the skin of his upper arm.

Noel reached for the thorn, covering his eyes as a flashlight glared into them.

He heard Ed's voice. "Hey, Little Miss Muffet, you're not trying to get out of here are you?"

Noel turned away from the light. "Just taking care of some business, Ed."

He blinked in the blaze of light, giving an apologetic shrug. "You know how it is."

Ed lowered the beam toward Noel's feet. "Yeah," he said, "I know exactly how that is." Ed's tone was ugly. "Now that you mention it, I've been doing some thinking about that," he said. "What kind of business are you in, Noel, just exactly?"

Noel shook his head. "Oh, you know, this and that."

Better to be vague, Noel thought.

Anything to get Ed off his back.

Ed tightened his lips and thumped the flashlight in his hands.

"That shit in there where you camp out... It's hot, right?"

Noel felt his breath tighten. "What makes you say that?"

"Instinct," Ed said.

Noel heard the venom in Ed's voice.

How did Ed know what he had in his place?

"I just got to thinking that you had some unusual things."

"Not much, really," Noel said.

"Not much, my ass," Ed said. "I got friends downtown might like to take a good look at all that stuff."

Noel put his hand on the car door.

"Put your hand down," Ed said. "I'm not done talking. Don't be rude."

"What are you getting at?" Noel said.

"I'm getting at this, asshole," Ed moved closer to Noel. "I know what you owe my mother. You bring that tomorrow, or you got problems."

Noel tried to speak, but crumpled under the force of Ed's flashlight driving into his gut.

For a second, Noel couldn't move as the world reeled around him.

He finally pulled himself up and worked his way

back to the car. He put his hand up to the Volvo's door.

Ed pulled the flashlight back and brought the cylinder down on Noel's hand with a chilling force.

"Don't think about messing with me," Ed said.

Noel lay on the ground, holding his hand in agony.

Ed stood above him, patting the flashlight in his palm.

"Don't even think about it."

THE
ALEXANDRITE

"I have to take the soufflé out," Tallie said.

She stood up, dropping her napkin on her chair.

"You said you had something to tell me," Page said.

Tallie's expression was a blank canvas.

"I did?"

What had Tallie planned to tell Page?

Page had wondered about it yesterday and today, hoping Tallie's news was a real position at the gallery.

"You did," Page said.

Tallie shook her head. "Come in the kitchen with me. I can't imagine what you're talking about."

Tallie was wearing the Alexandrite.

Hadn't Tallie hinted that the ring would be Page's someday? Page was certain that she had done exactly that.

Page had even dared to imagine Tallie might give her the ring tonight.

The Alexandrite was the most fabulous thing in

the world.

Obviously this wasn't the night.

How could she have even considered that? The only way to pry something away from Tallie was with a crowbar.

Tallie stood in the kitchen.

"Can I help?" Page asked.

"Darling..." Tallie said.

Tallie even made the apron she wore look elegant.

"You're such a dear to ask, but everything is ready now."

Tallie took the ring off her finger and placed it on the side of the sink.

"On the phone," Page said. "You said you had something to discuss with me. Something important."

Tallie shook her head. "I can't imagine what it was."

Holding a potholder, she pulled a soufflé from the oven.

"Carefully, carefully," Tallie cautioned herself.

Nothing, Page thought.

No job... Certainly no ring.

"These fall so easily, " she said to Page. "This wouldn't be the first."

* * *

"Another prize-winner," Walker said, wiping the corner of his mouth.

Tallie beamed. "You flatter me, Walker."

"How about the dishes?" Page asked. "May I help with them?"

They stacked the dishes on the counter next to the sink.

"Leave everything," Tallie said. "I'll have the girls do them tomorrow."

Tallie left the kitchen.

The ring was still beside the sink.

I could be suffering temporary insanity, Page thought.

Why shouldn't she just take it?

She wouldn't be stealing the ring.

Page simply wanted to know what it was worth.

She had talked to the woman at the gallery about appraising some things. A few unused wedding gifts. Things she never used.

But the ring would be hers someday.

Tallie had promised her the ring.

It would be nice to know the ring's value.

The Alexandrite lay precariously close to the sink, shimmering in the kitchen's bright light.

It would be a shame, Page thought, if the ring were to fall down into the disposal.

She picked up the ring. The color changed in various lights.

Right now it was a cloudy purple.

Someday it would be hers.

She looked around the kitchen.

She was alone.

Page dropped the ring into her pocket.

NEIGHBORS

Ed pressed his sensor onto the keypad at the Casa Solana Apartments.

Noel needs to start rolling his quarters, Ed thought.

The amount he owed Gladys for rent would cover Sawyer's retainer.

Remembering this fact lifted Ed's spirits.

The gate opened, allowing Ed entry into the tan stucco complex.

"Hey stranger," Eileen waved at Ed from her pool-side chaise.

Her terry bathrobe barely draped her bikini. "Coming in or out?"

Ed brushed the top of his shirt.

It's pretty cold, he thought.

"I'm coming in for now," he said.

"What's that 'for now' supposed to mean?"

She picked up the pitcher next to her.

"Get a glass, big guy. You like margaritas, don't you?"

"Where's your lover boy?" Ed asked.

He didn't like the idea of getting too cozy with Eileen if her boyfriend wasn't accounted for.

Not that the guy looked that tough, Ed just didn't like the idea of being caught by surprise.

"He took a powder."

Eileen poured a margarita into a plastic tumbler.

"Tis the season," she said, handing the drink toward Ed.

"Taste this. I really want to know what you think."

Ed took the tumbler from Eileen and sipped the drink.

"It's fine," he said.

"Ricky took off for the airport," Eileen said. "He won't be coming back tonight."

She adjusted herself against the beach towel on the chaise, lifted her knee, and threw her head back.

She gave Ed a dramatic look.

"So, here I am."

Ed sat down on the chaise next to Eileen.

"I've been meaning to get to know you better," he said. "Just to be neighborly, you know."

"That's cute," Eileen said. She took the margarita back from Ed and filled it to the brim. "Neighborly. That is so sweet."

She gave Ed a long look, covering his entire body in a smoldering glance.

The look lasted a little too long for Ed's taste.

He felt embarrassed.

Finally, she took her eyes off him.

She giggled.

"So, Ed, how long have you been a cop?"

* * *

Ed liked Eileen's laugh. It originated somewhere low in her vocal chords and Ed thought it was sexy. On his third margarita, he told her so.

"Anybody ever say you got a sexy way of laughing?"

"Yeah?" she said, interested. "It's just the way I laugh. I guess I've always laughed that way."

She laughed again.

This time self-consciously.

"Yeah," Ed said. "Like that. Nice and low. I like that."

Eileen gave an exaggerated frown, and held her belly. "Ho, ho, ho…" she said, "maybe I should get a job at the mall as Santa."

Ed wanted to take his time before suggesting they go inside.

"You could be Mrs. Claus, anyway."

Eileen looked shocked. "What, only men get to be the big cheese?"

"Hey," Ed said, "I didn't mean it that way. You want to be Santa, go ahead. Be my guest."

Eileen put her hand on Ed's arm.

Squeezed it hard.

"Relax," she said, "I was kidding."

* * *

"So why did you think I was a cop?" Ed asked. The pitcher of margaritas was almost empty and Ed had taken off his shoes.

Eileen worked her fingers into the stretchy band at the top of Ed's nylon socks.

"A wild guess," she said.

∗ ∗ ∗

"You should give it a try," she said. "The pay's good and the work isn't hard."

"I don't know," Ed said, "I'll think about it."

The idea of working security at a strip bar didn't appeal to Ed.

The fringe benefits might be good, but it was too much like a fulfillment of Roy Burns's prediction.

"Think about it," she said. "I can put in a good word for you."

She ran the edge of her fingernail across Ed's bicep.

"You'd be a shoo-in."

Ed put his hand over Eileen's.

"And from what you tell me," she said, "you need a job."

That was true. Ed would be out on the street in the new year.

What would he do then?

∗ ∗ ∗

"So," Eileen said, "how did you know that I was a dancer?"

In the dark, the lights surrounding the pool turned the water a phosphorescent green.

Eileen pursed her lips and pulled her bathrobe around herself for warmth.

Ed didn't answer. He put his arm under her waist and explored her neck with his lips.

"Come on," she said, pushing him slightly away. "How did you know?"

Ed brought his head level with Eileen's and looked directly in her eyes.

"Training," he said.

From the balcony, a man's voice bellowed.

Eileen jumped. Unwrapping herself from Ed, she knocked over what was left of the pitcher.

"What's the matter," Ed said.

"Can you disappear?" she hissed.

"I don't understand," Ed said.

"I gotta go," Eileen said, handing Ed his shoes. "We can talk some other time. I was serious about the job. We'll talk. I promise."

She cocked her head toward the balcony.

"Not now."

Ed put on his shoes. Slowly. He felt disoriented from the tequila and Eileen's abrupt behavior.

"Hurry up," she whispered. "It's Ricky."

Ed tried to grab her wrist.

He stared as Eileen pulled away from him and disappeared into the dark.

* * *

Ed woke up freezing next to the pool. The lights around the vivid green water were still on for security.

The glow wasn't nearly as romantic as it had been earlier.

Ricky was the boyfriend.

Ed had gotten a glimpse of the guy several days before. He looked like a cruiser-weight Fort Knox.

Like I need this kind of trouble, Ed thought.

He glanced at his watch. The light-up dial was the same color as the pool.

Eleven.

Earlier than he thought.

Ed rubbed his jaw.

Had Ricky seen him with Eileen?

Not that Ricky scared him, but Ed decided he needed to be careful about Eileen.

She could mean trouble.

CHESHIRE CAT SMILE

Wendell watched Rosemary putting out signs for the yard sale.

Maybe she would get some early morning traffic, he thought.

Wednesday was an odd day for a yard sale, Wendell thought, but Christmas was this weekend.

Wendell was happy Rosemary was putting the sale on.

Anything to get rid of her clutter.

Really, Wendell hadn't paid much attention to Rosemary's sale.

Tom's painting was all that he could think about.

How much was Tom's painting worth?

Tom didn't seem to have two nickels to rub together, but he had a fortune on his living room wall.

Did Tom know how much the painting was worth? If he did, wouldn't he have sold it long ago?

Wendell watched as Rosemary pulled out

unopened boxes from the back room.

There had to be a way to help Tom.

Tom was a harmless old guy, Wendell thought, and obviously he couldn't help himself.

Rosemary smiled at Wendell.

"I read in the paper this morning that if you haven't used something for over a year, you should get rid of it."

The idea sounded reasonable to Wendell.

"Wonderful," he said. "Go to it."

The yard sale might keep Rosemary occupied with something other than her writing.

"Do you want to help me price anything?"

Rosemary held a spool of twine in one hand and a pair of scissors in the other.

A box of paperbacks lay in front of her.

Dust-catchers, Wendell thought.

"No," he said. "You go ahead."

If only Wendell could help Tom.

Wendell finished his coffee, took the mug to the sink and ran it under hot water.

He smiled at Rosemary.

"You hold down the fort," he said. "I'm going over to talk to Tom."

* * *

"Oh, the painting," Tom said.

He looked surprised to see Wendell coming back so soon.

"That painting's got some history in it."

Amazing, Wendell thought. How could Tom be so blasé? The painting was worth a fortune.

Even if you didn't know anything about art, you would recognize a Maxwell Day.

"It's a Maxwell Day, isn't it?"

"Come in." Tom said, motioning for Wendell to enter.

"I'll show it to you, close up."

*   *   *

"It's unbelievable," Wendell muttered.

Tom took the painting down from the wall.

The painting was remarkable. A cavalry officer and an Indian sat together next to a campfire passing a peace pipe.

"You know who they are?" Tom said, pointing at the figures in the painting.

"No idea," Wendell said. "Probably one of the officers at Fort Lowell?"

Tom shook his head. "That's not what I mean."

He took his finger and traced a track of dust on the frame.

"I mean, you know who the people are, in the picture?"

It was exasperating. The old man was trying to make some point about the history behind the painting.

"Well," Wendell said, pointing at the Indian.

"He's not an Apache, that's for sure. Wrong clothing."

Tom laughed. "You don't recognize me, do you?"

Wendell looked from the old man to the painting, then back.

Time had passed of course, but Wendell could see that Tom had posed for the picture.

"Wow," Wendell said. "You must have known him well."

"Well enough," Tom said. "He was my neighbor for a while. You ever seen any pictures of him?"

"Maxwell Day?" Wendell said. "I don't think I have."

"He was a good looking cuss," Tom said. "But you look at that soldier there." He pointed at the cavalry officer in the painting. "That's what Max looked like at the time he painted this thing."

Wendell suppressed a gasp. "So it's a self-portrait, too."

"Yep," Tom said with evident pride. "Me on one side of the fire, Max on the other."

"Tom," Wendell said, "have you ever had this appraised?"

Tom looked at the painting. "Why would I do that? It's not for sale."

"Of course," Wendell said, quickly. "It's got sentimental value, I'm sure."

"Not just that," Tom said. "It's probably worth some real money."

Wendell tried hiding his excitement. "That's probably true. You should get an exact figure. Get it insured…"

Wendell held back, not wanting to go too far.

Tom might be skittish.

"Another thing you might want to consider…"

"Hold it." Tom held his palm toward Wendell. "I haven't considered the first part, yet."

Wendell frowned.

"That's all right. I was just thinking out loud. It's an incredible work."

Tom squinted.

"How much do you think it's worth?"

Wendell shook his head. "I don't have any idea. But if you did want to sell… I think it might make you very comfortable."

"Hell," Tom said. "I'm comfortable now. I got everything I need."

The old man gestured around at the sparse furnishings of his living room.

"Sure," Wendell said. "But maybe you could help out some of your family."

Tom looked thoughtfully at the painting.

"How would I get it appraised?"

Wendell gave a Cheshire cat smile.

"I can help you with that. I know a guy who does that kind of thing."

"Thanks anyway," Tom said.

He held the door open for Wendell.

"I'd just as soon stay in the dark."

THE CHESS GAME

Tom greeted Trinity at the Presidio Market.

"Sit down," Tom said.

The morning paper, folded on the seat next to Tom showed the lopsided score of the previous night's basketball game.

Tom, his heavy tortoise shell glasses perched on his nose, worked on a crossword puzzle in the newspaper.

Lesley smiled at Trinity.

"Are you ready for this?"

Lesley liked Tom. She thought he looked like John Wayne. "When do you head out?"

Tom's eyebrows raised. "Right after this," he said. "I don't like driving at night."

Tom slapped the chair with the rolled up paper.

Trinity sat down, glad to see his neighbor.

He glanced at the paper. "Cats did a number last night, didn't they?"

Tom nodded. "They're finally looking like a team."

"They're young," Trinity said. "The question is, are you ready?"

Tom nodded.

"Are you? Last chance before Christmas."

Trinity stood up, went behind the counter and took a mug from the rack.

He held up a carafe of coffee and pointed at Tom's mug. "Refill?"

Tom shook his head. "You're stalling."

Trinity grinned.

In a way, he was.

He pulled the chessboard out from under the counter and took the top from a wooden box. He held a white pawn and a black behind his back, and then pulled them around in front of himself.

Tom slapped Trinity's middle knuckle.

Trinity opened his hand slowly. Tom grinned at the sight of the white pawn.

"How come I never make you hold the pieces?" Trinity said.

Tom smiled again. "Rank has its privileges, doesn't it?"

Trinity nodded, concentrating on setting up the board. "I assumed it was age before beauty."

"That too," Tom said, pushing the first pawn forward.

❉ ❉ ❉

"Check and mate," Tom said, placing his knight down. Trinity's king couldn't move without going into check either from Tom's bishop or the rook he had slid all the way down the board several moves before.

"You played well, amigo," Tom said, nodding his head slightly toward Trinity.

Trinity had sensed defeat early in the game.

Tom had known as well.

A little lapse in Trinity's concentration, and the knight he planned to use as the spearhead of his attack was taken.

Trinity offered Tom his hand, and the older man accepted it.

"Another?" Trinity said.

Tom shook his head.

"Another day, of course I will. Right now, I'm going north. I gotta pay my respects to the Dutchman."

Trinity sipped his coffee. Was it rain he saw outside the window? He enjoyed playing chess with Tom.

Temperamentally, the two men were very similar.

Trinity started to set the chess pieces back on the board.

"Did what's-his-name bring you any of the luminarias?"

Lesley turned to look at Trinity from behind the counter.

"Frank, you didn't unleash Wendell on Tom, did you?"

Tom looked quizzically at Trinity. "You sent him?"

Trinity shook his head. "I said I'd give you some

of the bags. He insisted on doing it himself."

"That's tonight, isn't it?" Tom looked as if he was trying to remember something.

"Until Christmas," Lesley said. "It's going to be beautiful. We need to take a walk through the neighborhood."

"Your friend's a little…" Tom squinted and held his hand out and wiggled it from side to side.

"Different?" Lesley said.

"That's putting it kindly," Tom said. "I meant to say something a little stronger. Maybe in Spanish."

"Don't hold back on my account," Trinity said.

"You know what he used to do?" Tom placed his fingers along the lip of his cup.

"More coffee?" Trinity said.

Tom nodded. "He was a teacher, of some sort. God help us."

"Guidance counselor," Lesley said.

"Frightening, isn't it," Trinity said.

Tom handed the cup toward Trinity. "Just a half. I don't want to disturb my siesta. He's very excited though. He thinks that he's doing me a huge favor."

"Something about the luminarias?" Trinity said.

"No," Tom said. "That was nothing. He couldn't stop looking at my painting."

"Painting?" Trinity said. He didn't remember any painting in Tom's house.

"You don't know what I'm talking about?" Tom waited until Trinity returned with the coffee. "It's right in the middle of the living room. You might not have noticed it."

Trinity shook his head. "I guess I don't remember seeing it."

Tom shrugged.

"Sam Spade. Oh well, Wendell thinks it's worth a fortune. That's what he told me. He offered to get it appraised."

"Interesting," Trinity said. "I wouldn't think he had any time to spare from the luminarias."

Tom laughed. "We'll see. It's a nice old painting. A friend of mine painted it years ago. I told him that I'd never sell it."

"You don't remember that painting?" Lesley looked surprised. "It's gorgeous."

Trinity shook his head. "My powers of observation..."

"They're shot," Lesley said.

"I am a little curious how much the thing's worth," Tom said. "I should probably insure it."

"Come on," Trinity said. "Another game. I insist." He turned the board around. "This time I've got white."

"That's going to make a difference?" Lesley said.

"Please," Tom said, holding his index finger in the air, "Lew Archer is an optimist. Let's not discourage him.

✳ ✳ ✳

"Checkmate," Tom said.

Almost apologetically.

"I should tell you, there was a time when I did

almost nothing but play chess. Guard duty."

Trinity shook his head. "You used your time well."

Tom stood up. "The company was swell. I hope you brought enough money to pay for the coffee."

Trinity laughed. "Don't worry. The day that I beat you, I'll let you buy me a steak."

Tom laughed. "That'll be the day."

"So you're gone for how long?" Trinity asked.

With his weathered face, and his drawl, Tom did look like John Wayne.

"A day or so," he said, heading toward the door. "Unless I strike gold."

❈ ❈ ❈

The sun reflected through the glass of the Presidio Market.

"Dinner?" Trinity said.

"Let me get a few things together, Frank," she said, smiling.

She stood at the doorway. They were the only ones in the market.

"Don't worry," she said. "I'll let you pay."

"I'll be back, then," he said, pausing in the doorway.

"Promises, promises."

BUILT UP TOXINS

Wendell couldn't believe Tom. Some people simply didn't recognize it when you did them a favor.

Wendell had a plan. If Tom didn't know what was good for him, Wendell would have to go ahead and take care of business for him.

The guy down the street could appraise the painting.

What was his name? Jeremy... That was it. Jeremy Powers. The one with the wife.

Wendell had stopped into their store a couple of times. The place was always deserted. Jeremy would certainly have time to do a favor for a neighbor.

If Tom decided to sell, Wendell would handle everything. The value would probably be more money than Tom could turn down.

Wendell looked down the street at Tom's house.

A half an hour passed before Tom left his house. What had Trinity said?

Tom would be gone for a couple of days.

Trinity would know how long. Wasn't he some kind of detective?

* * *

Wendell lugged the painting into his house, propping it on a living room chair.

"What have you got there?" Rosemary said.

"This is Tom's," Wendell said.

* * *

A job well done, Wendell thought.

He piled mesquite limbs into the burn box of the sweat lodge. Building the sweat lodge was the first thing he did after he and Rosemary moved in. Wendell was practically an expert in Native American healing ceremonies.

He would get Jeremy to appraise the painting.

Wendell lit a twisted section of newspaper. Something about a basketball game. He would heat the rocks and then pour cold water on them.

Jeremy would be at the store. There would be enough time for Jeremy to appraise the painting before Tom returned home.

Tomorrow, Wendell would crawl into the little space and let the steam from the rocks cover his body.

Tom would never know the painting had been borrowed.

Wendell depended on the sweat lodge. The steam would release all his built up toxins.

A FAVOR FROM FENTON

Fenton didn't like talking on the phone.

"Make it fast," Fenton said.

"I'm asking you a favor," Noel said.

He was wheedling again, just like he had with Gladys.

Noel hated being in this position.

He glanced out the window.

In her yard Gladys fumbled with a string of Christmas lights.

Begging from Fenton was beneath his dignity, but Noel couldn't think of any alternative.

"A favor," Fenton said.

Noel pictured Fenton on the other end of the line.

Fenton would still be in his bathrobe, probably scratching himself.

"Like the other favors I've done for you?" Fenton's voice alternated between oil and gravel.

Either way, it sounded condescending.

Fenton always held the better hand and he

always knew it.

"When are you paying me back for all the other favors?"

Gladys brought a ladder to the front of the house.

"I can pay you back," Noel said.

Fenton couldn't resist the urge to turn the knife in Noel's flesh.

Noel held the phone under his chin and cracked his knuckles. How could he convince Fenton? There had to be something he could do for him.

Some job that would get Gladys to call off her son.

"I swear I can pay you back. You gotta have something for me."

Fenton's laugh turned into a long coughing spasm. Noel covered the phone. Fenton's laugh was a good sign. At least Fenton wasn't angry. Fenton was thinking things over.

Noel idly turned on the classical music station on his radio, turning the volume low.

"Hang tight," Fenton said. "You never know what might turn up."

"I need some money," Noel said.

He hated Fenton's game of cat and mouse.

Fenton started to laugh again.

"I said, wait and see what I come up with. That's all I can do."

Noel felt better. Fenton hadn't given him a complete turndown.

Fenton would give him a job. Fenton always kept his word.

It didn't make sense to wait for Fenton to call.

Fenton might not need him for months at a time.

Noel would need to come up with an alternate plan.

He turned the radio up.

The music sounded majestic.

If he went out again tonight, Noel thought, he would probably make enough to buy some food.

Not nearly enough for the rent.

He had a five in his pocket.

Good for tuna fish, at least.

Noel could still feel where Ed's fist had driven into his gut.

If he didn't come up with some money he would have to move.

Noel hated the idea of finding a new place.

Noel always took pains to slip into the background, to go unnoticed. Ed's threats changed that. He didn't know what to do.

The music from the radio reached a crescendo.

Tympani announced the end.

THE EAGLE
TALON

Rosemary Gentry filled another box for the yard sale. Wendell liked her to declutter the house.

On her own, Rosemary would keep everything.

But she also enjoyed the money these sales generated.

The yard sales also gave her a chance to talk to different people. Everybody said it was important for a writer to listen to people.

She looked at the painting Wendell brought from Tom's house.

Not bad, she thought. Obviously, Wendell intended for her to sell it.

She pulled out the roll of masking tape from her apron pocket.

Well, she wouldn't just give the painting away.

She squinted at the painting. The men were both quite handsome.

The painting would make a good book cover, Rosemary thought.

She looked again, this time more critically.

It would be even better if there was an attractive woman in the painting, maybe seated between the two men.

As a writer, Rosemary liked to provide a narrative, and a woman between the two handsome men would have done just that.

* * *

A stroke of luck, Jeremy thought.

He looked at the painting.

Right here, practically on the street.

At a yard sale of all places.

A magnificent stroke of luck.

He'd almost tripped over the painting.

Unbelievable, Jeremy thought.

It was the real thing.

Jeremy looked again.

The talon was right where it was supposed to be.

Maxwell Day always painted an eagle talon into the lower right-hand corner of his paintings.

It was an original, flawless, Maxwell Day.

Going to the gallery reception had paid off.

It was more than simply an opportunity to eat hors d'oeuvres and drink a couple of glasses of wine.

Even if he hadn't gone to the gallery, Jeremy would have recognized that this painting was valuable.

It was a well-deserved stroke of luck.

Long overdue.

Jeremy tried to keep calm.

"Such a lovely picture, isn't it?" the woman said.

She had stuck masking tape on the frame and marked a price of fifty dollars.

Fifty dollars.

The woman probably thought she was pushing her luck.

Things like this never happen, Jeremy thought.

How many yard sales had he been to?

"I'll work with you on that price."

The woman was all business, probably mistaking Jeremy's shock in discovering the painting for a reluctance to buy.

"The fifty dollars includes the frame," she added.

Jeremy carefully picked the painting up from the chair on which it was placed.

She has no idea, he thought.

Jeremy pulled his wallet out slowly, careful not to betray his excitement.

"It's kind of nice," he said. "Why not?"

Rosemary smiled, concentrating while counting the bills.

Why not, indeed, Jeremy thought, looking at the picture again.

It was perfect.

The paintings in the gallery had been impressive, but this one outdid them.

A cavalry officer sharing a peace pipe with an Apache warrior.

Maxwell Day.

Perhaps his masterpiece.

OUTSIDE CARUSO'S

Bathed in the light of Caruso's neon sign, Trinity and Lesley watched the man in the velvet jacket.

Holding his hands in the air and with his head craned upward, the man darted back and forth, in and out of the dark shadow between the sidewalk and the building.

He was pointing upwards.

Something was falling.

The man slid invisible furniture out of the way. His hair fell into his whitened face.

His mouth gaped in shocked suprise.

A few people watching him glanced nervously upward.

The falling object had to be the size of a baby grand.

The man in the velvet jacket staggered around the cement sidewalk, his scuffed brown wingtips outlining a cockeyed circle.

The falling object took forever, but only a few of the spectators had thrown money into the man's derby hat.

The man in the velvet jacket abruptly stopped his whirling and signaled the end of the act with an abrupt clap.

A few of the people, milling around the front of the restaurant waiting to be seated, turned toward him.

With only a few eyes upon him, the man sprang into a handstand, walking on the edge of the sidewalk before stopping in front of the restaurant door.

Trinity dropped a couple of bills into the derby before holding the door of Caruso's open for Lesley.

The man in the velvet jacket, still in the handstand, made eye contact with Trinity, who nodded in appreciation.

"Live theater," Trinity said.

"Isn't he good?" Lesley said. "Sometimes he performs in front of the market. Everyone loves him."

"There's more to the act than that, I hope."

Trinity wasn't sure how long the man could sustain interest in an audience by relying on the piano-catching bit.

"I mean, what does he do for an encore?"

"What do any of us do," Lesley said.

She looked playful, but by her tone Trinity could tell she was being serious.

"I mean, we run around trying the best we can to catch things that are falling out of the sky... Don't we?"

She looked at Trinity as if to gain support.

The hostess took them to their table.

"I don't know," Trinity said. "Most of the time I've got my head down."

＊ ＊ ＊

They walked from Trinity's Bronco to the door of Lesley's apartment.

"Dinner was lovely, Frank," Lesley said.

"It was nice," Trinity said.

"I forgot to say what I was concerned about."

"You were concerned?"

Lesley leaned against Trinity. He felt her body against his.

"I think you should watch out for Wendell. I'm not sure he has Tom's best interests at heart."

"Are you kidding?" Trinity said. "That guy doesn't have anyone's interests at heart but his own."

Lesley raised her eyebrows.

"What about Tom?"

"Tom?" Trinity shook his head. "I wouldn't worry about Tom."

Lesley didn't look convinced.

Trinity touched Lesley's forehead.

"Try playing chess with him sometime."

PEACE PIPE

Jeremy put the painting down on a chair in the living room and stared at it in the light from the picture window.

Sinking down opposite the painting, he pulled the bottle out from behind the recliner.

He could look at the painting forever. The sunset featured the rich shades of blues and oranges for which Maxwell Day was famous. In the foreground, the cavalry officer accepted the peace pipe from an Indian.

They sat next to a fire which blazed with such intensity that Jeremy could almost smell the smoke.

Jeremy filled a tumbler with ice and splashed whiskey over the top.

He swirled the drink then held it toward the painting.

"Here's to you," he said. "There's none like you."

AN APPEALING FUTURISTIC QUALITY

Rosemary stared at the mesquite vigas on the ceiling. Working the red rubber tip of the eraser against her full lower lip, she counted the ribs.

It was meditation for the end of a day.

Restful and energizing.

A very successful day, she thought.

The money from the sale gave her extra money for Christmas.

Of course, Wendell would have to give Tom the money for his painting.

Rosemary smiled.

She was happy they were able to help their neighbor.

The two pages of her story gleamed brilliantly.

She congratulated herself.

She looked through the slats in her window. Gladys's renter pulled into the driveway. Rosemary couldn't remember his name. It was something unusual, she was sure of that.

She picked up her pen and wrote a phrase in bold, green, calligraphic script. Finishing the last word, Rosemary sketched a circle around the words, and then sketched bubbles between the circle and the letters.

The bubbles gave the sentence a futuristic quality Rosemary found appealing.

The two pages were terrific. She wouldn't need a second draft.

Rosemary pushed her harlequin glasses to the broad dome of her forehead. Why did so many people insist on rewriting?

Rosemary never felt the need to rewrite.

She rarely mentioned her writing to Wendell. When he was being generous, Wendell called Rosemary's writing naïve and childish.

Wendell had disappeared after bringing in the painting.

He was probably getting ready for one of his sweats.

Noel.

That was the man's name.

Noel Brisbane.

Call me Brisbane, Rosemary thought.

Now that was an excellent line.

As a writer, Rosemary had to gauge people's emotions. In her professional estimation, Noel was nervous most of the time.

Rosemary looked out the window into the side yard. She could see most of Noel's house. Noel stood in the front yard.

Rosemary looked back at the vigas. The mesquite ribs were smoky brown. They contrasted nicely with the light cocoa color of the interior walls.

Wendell had chosen the color scheme. His taste was impeccable.

She paused, holding her pen in midair.

Seeing Noel made her wonder again.

It was a nagging question, and Rosemary worried it like a loose tooth.

She couldn't decide.

Should she tell anyone about Ed sneaking into Noel's house?

* * *

The scream startled her. She'd never heard Wendell sound like that.

He burst through the door, his face contorted in rage.

Rosemary turned to him.

"What the hell did you do with the painting?" Wendell screamed.

AN UNSPOKEN CODE

Another day, Margo thought.

Another day had come and gone with no customers.

She was about to close the shop when the phone rang.

The call from Page surprised Margo.

"I've got something," Page said. "I really, really need an appraisal."

"Sure," Margo said. "That's not a problem. What do you have?"

Margo hadn't expected to see or hear from Page. The conversation about appraisals had only been chit-chat.

Wouldn't the Day Gallery have its own appraisers?

Of course it would.

"An Alexandrite," Page said. "I really need it in a hurry."

As if that made any difference, Margo thought.

"Nice," Margo said, "We'd love to do it. I'll be here all day tomorrow."

"I really have to have it done quickly," Page said. "It's complicated."

"That's all right," Margo said. "I'm just closing up here. How about we meet at my house? I'll eyeball it, then if you need something written, Jeremy can write it up later."

Margo hoped that she could do something with Jeremy while Page was there. She was glad Page had called. It might even be nice to have her as a friend.

❊ ❊ ❊

"You did what?" Wendell screamed.

Rosemary stared at her husband. She had never seen him this upset.

"I told you everything, Wendell. I don't know what else to say."

"What did he look like?" Wendell shouted.

Rosemary shook her head. "I told you," she said, "I really wasn't paying attention. I must have been doing something else."

Wendell turned away from her and slapped the wall next to the door. "You better remember fast."

Rosemary shook her head. Tears came to her eyes.

She was a writer. She should be able to remember what the man looked like.

"I'm sorry," she said. "I am so sorry. I just can't

remember."

* * *

Page held the ring.

What had she been thinking of? Had she lost her mind?

She shrugged. There was nothing to do except let Margo or her husband appraise it.

Sooner or later the ring really would belong to her.

She might as well find out it's value.

How would she get it back to Tallie?

Page rubbed the ring like a worry stone.

Page couldn't sneak into Tallie's house uninvited.

That would go against an unspoken code. It would be worse than embarrassing to be caught sneaking into Tallie's house.

That would be unforgivable.

Tallie might not notice that the ring was missing.

Page glanced at her watch.

She had to wait.

It would take a while for Margo to get home.

Everything would be fine.

Margo or her husband could tell at a glance how much the ring was worth.

Page certainly didn't want anything in writing.

Then she would just take the ring back to Tallie's house.

Somehow she would take it back.

Page went to her closet and took out her winter coat.

She twirled once in front of the hall mirror, admiring her reflection.

Lipstick, she thought.

She pulled out her purse.

Page put the ring in a small velvet box she found after getting home from Tallie's.

She had to take one more look at the ring.

Each facet of the gem was delightful.

She etched the bright red lipstick and looked at herself again.

She put on the ring.

She had thought of wearing the ring to bed last night.

She smiled. Even Walker would have noticed that.

Maybe.

She glanced again at the ring and regretfully took it off.

The setting was no great prize.

She would definitely have it re-set.

* * *

The phone rang.

It was Walker.

"Tallie called me. It's about her ring. She thinks one of the cleaning ladies took it."

"My God," Page said. "The Alexandrite? That's terrible. When was the last time she saw it?"

Walker sounded impatient. "Who knows?"

"She should call the plumbers." Page said. "It's probably trapped in a drain."

She paused and took a deep breath.

"There's no way Inez would ever take anything," Page said, "or the other one either."

Page pictured the two women.

Inez and her sister, who's name Page never could remember.

It would be awful if Tallie thought they stole her ring.

She had to get it back quickly.

"Walker," she said. "I'm going out. I've got errands."

"When are you going to be home?" Walker said.

She could hear it in his voice.

He didn't trust her.

* * *

Page got in the Volkswagen.

Finding Margo's house would be easy.

Page couldn't take the ring to the shop.

No, it would be better to do this very casually.

Just have Margo take a look at the ring at her house.

She steered the Volkswagen out of her driveway.

Christmas lights would be coming on soon and they would shine through the cacti in front of the houses.

Page's home in Colonia Solana was as close to authentic Sonoran Desert as you would find in the center of town.

It wouldn't take a minute for them to look at the ring.

What was Margo's husband's name?

Page searched her memory. She remembered seeing him at the reception.

Jeremy.

That was it. Just like Chad and Jeremy.

What was the name of their song?

The lights were lovely. A blaze of red and green before she turned on Country Club. The sun dropped below the horizon.

An oncoming car honked.

Page twisted the knob to turn the car's lights on. Funny she hadn't thought to do so earlier.

The oncoming car swerved quickly.

Somebody's in a hurry, Page thought.

It was a near miss.

Everybody's out doing Christmas shopping.

What do you get for Walker? Or Tallie, for that matter?

Page dug into her purse, groping for the ring. She kept one hand on the steering wheel while recalling the conversation she had with Walker.

The loss of the ring was bad, Page thought, but not the end of the world.

Insurance would cover it.

She winced. Of course, insurance would cover the loss.

The ring would be stolen property.

Page didn't want that to happen.

She wanted to keep the ring.

If it were stolen, she would never be able to wear it.

And she would be a thief.

At Ina, she turned the overhead lights on in the car and checked the directions Margo had given her.

She hoped that Margo would be home. Margo was a sympathetic person.

In the French sense, Page thought.

God, Page thought, high school French...

Margo est sympathique.

Driving alone in the Tucson twilight, Page looked forward to speaking with someone sympathique.

RUST ORANGE
RECLINER

Typical behavior for Jeremy, Margo thought, driving from the shop to her house.

Naturally, he wouldn't just answer the phone, preferring instead to let the answering machine take the calls.

Even the message irritated Margo. Jeremy's breathless remarks implied that he was out evaluating some fabulous estate.

Margo expected Jeremy to be comatose. Wasn't it the same every night? Tonight was no exception. The empty whiskey bottle lay on its side at his feet. Jeremy was sprawled in the rust orange recliner. Inert. Slack-jawed. Curly hair matted against the fabric of the chair.

A vision, Margo thought.

Jeremy could identify a fake at forty paces and could distinguish between obscure sterling patterns at a glance.

Look at him, she thought.

Margo barely noticed the painting. Margo had

grown accustomed to Jeremy spending much of his life in a semi-catatonic state.

He could die like this, Margo thought.

How would she feel if he died?

She shook her head, looking at her husband. Would she feel disloyal? Guilty?

Margo glanced at the painting.

Oh, my God, she thought. What has he done?

She lunged for the painting on the chair. It frightened Margo.

What had Jeremy done? She hadn't believed that he would actually do it.

Jeremy could have been dead. He didn't respond to Margo's shaking.

"Wake the hell up," Margo shouted.

No response. She slapped him on the upper part of his arm, hard enough that she knew a welt would appear.

In this condition I could hold a pillow over his face...

Get hold of yourself, she thought.

The bleary lid of Jeremy's right eye opened, and quickly closed seeing his wife's indignant form. Jeremy's mouth made a soundless grimace and he touched his arm.

"Don't play with me, Jeremy. I mean it."

Margo grabbed Jeremy's face with both hands and pointed it toward the painting.

"Why did you do it?" she shouted.

The Indian in the painting was frozen, passing the pipe to the cavalry officer.

My God, Margo thought, we are finished.

She looked at Jeremy. His head slumped toward his shoulder.

He'll be like this for hours, she thought.

She had to make him wake up. Jeremy was as far gone as she had ever seen him.

She found the phone book.

Jeremy stole the painting, but she refused to let him profit from it.

She knew she had to call Fenton. It would take courage to call him, but Margo couldn't think of an alternative. Just looking at the painting gave Margo a sick feeling. She couldn't have it in the house; they would say she was as culpable as Jeremy.

They would call her an accessory after the fact. Something like that, anyway.

It would be her luck to take a fall for Jeremy.

She wouldn't let it happen.

Jeremy wouldn't win. Margo wouldn't let him.

She picked up the phone. Matthew Fenton would be a start.

✳ ✳ ✳

"I'll be there in half an hour," Margo said.

Fenton hung up the phone.

"By the way, Stella," Fenton said to his housekeeper. "I have a guest arriving in a bit. Why don't you scoot out when she gets here?"

Stella pursed her lips and nodded.

What would Stella think of Margo? Fenton didn't want the housekeeper around when he talked to Margo. The conversation with Margo stirred up emotions for Fenton. Hadn't he gotten over Tallie? It was ludicrous, wasn't it?

Here he was, Fenton reminded himself, an old man. A rich old man, perhaps, but still an old man.

He should be over all that.

Water over the dam.

Why did he keep going back to the gallery?

Why did he act like a kid with his nose pressed against a window, hoping to get a glimpse of Tallie?

All of it had happened, when?

A hundred years ago?

The stories that he could tell Margo.

Margo...

Something about the sparkle in her eye reminded Fenton of Tallie.

Fenton opened his closet and pulled out a shirt.

Her husband was a fool.

Fenton had seen that right away.

Fenton shook his head. Some things weren't any easier to understand with age.

How could a person be foolish enough not to appreciate Margo?

It was an age-old question.

Once upon a time, he had wondered the same about Max Day and Tallie.

He looked at his hands, buttoning his shirt.

They looked like his father's hands.

Where had the time gone?

His shirt was dingy.

Even Stella was getting older.

Looking back in the closet, Fenton selected a freshly pressed striped shirt, and carefully inserted a pair of cufflinks he took from the leather box he kept on his dresser.

His father's cufflinks.

He was an old man, he thought, looking at the liver spots on the tops of his wrists.

He closed his eyes and could see the dark curls of hair and the sparkling green eyes that had once belonged to Tallie.

❊ ❊ ❊

Margo was uncomfortable.

Fenton helped her take off her coat, insisted on giving her a small glass of brandy, and refreshed his own. She wore the same dress and shoes she wore earlier in the day.

Would she be surprised that he noticed?

Even in a coma, he would notice Margo.

She sat on the couch, looking around his living room, eying the furniture and paintings with professional interest.

"Part of my collection," he said.

"You have beautiful taste," she said.

"I should blush, I suppose, but I gotta say that I agree."

The fact that Margo admired his taste was a tribute to her own.

"Do you mind me asking where some of these things came from?"

Fenton twisted the corner of his mouth. "I'd have to refer to notes."

Margo laughed. She was still obviously nervous, but doing her best not to show it.

"Sorry," she said, "I don't know where my manners have gone."

Fenton waved his hand. "Don't say another word about it. You were telling me something on the phone…"

Margo closed her eyes and let her head fall back against a cushion. "I have to apologize for my husband," she said.

Fenton laughed. "He certainly loved my paintings. I showed him these."

"These were the ones he saw?"

Fenton shrugged. "That's all of them."

Margo looked at the paintings on the wall. Fenton would notice if one were gone…

But the one in their house…

Margo tried to sound casual.

"You were telling me about the Day paintings. Do you know where most of them ended up?"

Fenton sipped the brandy. "Ended up?"

＊ ＊ ＊

"From the description, I'd have to say that it was done in the late fifties."

Fenton stopped, as if doing mental calculations.

"That was an interesting period. I'd like to see it."

Margo held the brandy in front of her and stared into the golden shadows within the glass.

She had barely taken a sip.

Fenton's eyes narrowed. "Of course the obvious question is where your husband got the painting."

Margo shook her head. "I hoped that you might know something about this painting. I thought you might know who it belonged to."

"You can't ask your husband?"

Fenton leaned forward, then put up his hands.

"Sorry," he said.

Fenton knew all about Jeremy.

"I don't know if he would tell me the truth."

Fenton nodded. "You have an approximate idea of the value of the painting, don't you?"

Margo sipped the brandy. "You saw me at the gallery."

"Of course." Fenton smiled. "What kind of service did you think I could provide?"

"Do you think the painting is stolen?"

Fenton held his hands up, fingers splayed. "That's a strong likelihood."

Margo looked crestfallen.

"I'll have to consider this, though," Fenton said. "I might need a little time."

He walked toward the sideboard. "More brandy?"

Margo shook her head.

Fenton lifted the stopper from the cut glass decanter, splashed some brandy into his own glass, swirled it.

"Do you want to make money on the painting?"

He waited for her reaction, deciding to let the words sink in.

What was she really here for, anyway? Of course, she would like that.

And better her than Jeremy.

Her eyes were red.

Margo's shoulders lifted slightly.

"Yes," she said.

A glimmer crossed Fenton's face.

"I might have a person who can help you," he said. "Let me make a phone call."

He left the room.

Margo sank deeper in the couch. What kind of Faustian bargain was Fenton offering?

The paintings and furniture in his house amazed her.

Jeremy must have been beside himself.

The house and furniture were fabulous.

Fabulous...

Page...

How had she managed to forget about Page?

ALI BABA

"I have an assignment for you."

Fenton's announcement was both quick and cryptic.

Noel stood barefoot on the chilly wooden floor of the studio, listening to Fenton's voice on the phone. Noel knew better than to ask Fenton for details. Fenton preferred to chart out assignments while Noel stood in front of him like a supplicant.

Noel's breath condensed in front of him, walking to the Volvo. Even for late December it was cold. Cold for Tucson, at any rate. Frost lined the bottom of the Volvo's windshield and Noel waited several minutes while the air pouring out of the heater turned warm. Noel checked his cash. A fiver and a few ones still in his pocket. A blessing, he thought. He didn't want to face Fenton on an empty stomach.

* * *

The waitress smiled at Noel, and poured him a cup of coffee. "Are you ready for Christmas?" she asked.

Noel raised his eyebrows.

"Ready as I'm going to get," he said.

"I'm not," the waitress said. "I've got a hundred things to do."

Did she really want to talk to him, Noel wondered, or was this just what she did? He glanced at the waitress. She stood poised with her pad.

Just making small talk, he decided.

"Cheeseburger," he said. "Can you put that on sourdough?"

"Not a problem," she said.

She brought the plate and filled his cup again.

"What do you have to do to get ready?" he said.

She rolled her eyes. "The usual," she said. "Too much to do, and not enough time in the day. I wouldn't be ready even if Christmas were in two weeks."

Noel nodded.

"And I don't want to disappoint my kid." She wiped a crumb from the table.

She's a beautiful woman, Noel thought. And she didn't want to disappoint her kid. Noel's problems were nothing. Noel pulled out his wallet, took the bills and flattened them on the side of the table.

Twelve dollars. When the waitress came back, he handed the money to her.

"I don't need change," he said. "Merry

Christmas."

Leaving the restaurant, Noel heard her thank him.

He was flat broke.

Maybe it would bring him luck.

＊ ＊ ＊

Fenton came back into the room.

"You say your husband's passed out, right?"

Margo nodded. "Jeremy won't wake up till around ten in the morning. A bomb could go off."

"Good," Fenton said. "I got a guy coming to pick it up."

He lifted his glass. "Better you should be away when he gets it."

Margo nodded.

"He'll be discreet," Fenton said. "You should stay away from the house though, for a couple more hours."

＊ ＊ ＊

Fenton offered Noel a cup of tea.

He's playing with me, Noel thought.

How long did it take me to get here? Now he offers me tea?

"I got some last minute instructions," Fenton said. "Ignore them at your own peril."

Noel shook his head and took a sip of the tea. "Go ahead and shoot," he said.

"It's nothing," Fenton said "just one tiny more thing." Fenton paused. It was one of Fenton's don't-mess-this-thing-up pauses. "You gotta do a perfect job."

Noel knew better than to interrupt Fenton, but he couldn't help wondering why the old man was going through all this.

Noel always did a perfect job. Always.

"One painting," Fenton said. "Nothing else. I want you to be like Ali Baba. You know what I mean. Don't take anything else from the place, no matter what you see."

"You know me," Noel said.

"That's what I'm worried about." Fenton said.

"Ignore the guy in the recliner," Fenton said, "He won't give you any trouble."

Noel cocked his head. What the hell was Fenton talking about?

"Just the damn painting, Noel," he said. "Like Ali Baba ... Nothing else."

Like Ali Baba, Noel thought.

Fenton's instructions were always clear.

But Ali Baba? Noel laughed.

Fenton was comparing him to an amateur.

GOLDILOCKS

Her conversation with Walker, combined with the near accident, upset Page.

Tallie knew the ring was missing. It was only a matter of time, Page thought, before Tallie connected the dots and accused Page of the theft.

There would be no chance of defending herself. She could see Walker's unforgiving, inflexible face in her mind's eye. Walker would not be able to find a way to excuse this. Both he and Tallie would assume that she had been drunk when she took the ring.

That might not be a bad idea, Page thought.

The way she was treated, why shouldn't she drink?

She could stage a preemptive strike.

If they discovered she had stolen the ring, Page would simply tell them that she had relapsed. It happened all the time.

At least that was what they said at the treatment center.

It would be shameful, but handing the ring back

under those circumstances might not be as bad as getting caught sneaking it back.

She was sober when she took the ring.

How do you go about explaining something like that?

Page toyed with the idea.

One drink. No more than that. She could control herself, of course.

One drink.

Maybe two...

She had been sober for more than a year.

She wouldn't allow herself to get completely out of control.

She gasped for breath.

Was she completely out of her mind?

No, she thought, far from it.

After what she had been through, she would be crazy not to have a drink.

She needed to get rid of the stress.

She needed a drink.

✳ ✳ ✳

Noel climbed back in the Volvo.

Fenton was a good person to know.

The job would be easy if it went the way Fenton had described it. Fenton tended toward broad strokes, and his instructions to Noel were impressionistic.

In any event, Noel was grateful.

With this job, he would have more than enough money to pay his rent to Gladys.

Things were looking up.

* * *

The man behind the counter barely looked up at Page entering the brightly lit liquor store. The neon signs cast pools of light onto the dark sidewalk near the dirt parking lot where Page had left the VW.

It's no big deal for him, Page thought. No need to explain anything to the guy.

Look at him, Page thought.

The man wore a blue sweatshirt and a cigarette hung from his mouth.

What on earth did the man care?

Don't start talking to him, Page told herself.

Don't say anything to him.

If she said anything, she would end up telling him the story of her life.

Telling him that she didn't intend to get drunk.

Telling him why she just needed one little drink.

She knew that the man at the counter wouldn't understand, or care.

Page looked at the video monitor and watched herself.

She looked fine.

Better than fine, in fact.

The man behind the counter didn't look up.

No offer of help.

Nothing.

She knew what she wanted.

She would buy something nobody would normally drink.

She found it in the center aisle near a seasonal display.

Just in time for Christmas.

❊ ❊ ❊

Noel's gut still felt sore.

Ed's flashlight had done a number.

He looked at himself in the rear view mirror, giving his uncooperative cowlick a swipe.

Getting out of the car, he hid in the bushes and peered through the window of the house.

He didn't have to dig deeply into his bag of tricks to get into the place. It would be easy for him.

The street and driveway in front were as quiet as they were dark.

The painting rested on a chair in the front part of the living room.

It was a good size, but it was still very manageable.

❊ ❊ ❊

Noel stood in front of the painting. An Indian and a cavalry officer sat on either side of a camp fire.

Noel was equal to the challenge.

The man in the recliner shook his head.

"You didn't," the man mumbled.

Noel glanced at him.

Talking in his sleep.

Noel watched the man for a couple of moments. The man's head lolled onto his shoulders.

Noel waved his hand experimentally in front of the man's face.

No response.

He examined the area surrounding the chair. No sign of a wire. He waved his hand in a circle around the painting, preparing to run if an electric eye sounded an alarm.

As if there would be one of those...

Noel looked over his shoulder. The man in the recliner assumed another position, this time with his head facing Noel. The palms of his hands lay upward at his sides and his legs splayed in front of him.

Not exactly an opportune position to start a forty yard dash, Noel thought.

He lifted the painting.

Noel glanced at the table next to the chair.

A wallet lay open.

Nice, Noel thought.

To hell with Ali Baba.

❉ ❉ ❉

Putting the bottle of Grand Marnier on the counter, Page smiled at the man.

"I'm making a soufflé," she said. "You need Grand Marnier for that."

The man behind the counter nodded and took her money.

❉ ❉ ❉

Noel picked up the wallet and thumbed through it.

No temptation here, he thought.

No cash or credit cards.

He pushed the wallet away.

❉ ❉ ❉

Pulling into Margo's driveway, Page felt embarrassed.

She wondered if coming here to Margo's house had been the right idea.

What right did she have to impose herself upon Margo? Margo's life was fine. The last thing that she needed was for Page to interfere.

The drink had made a big difference.

She looked at the bottle.

Grand Marnier…

Not bad.

Wonderful, in fact.

She still was in control, but she felt a lot more at ease.

Why on earth had she made such a production out of this?

She had two things going for her.

She felt so much better. Like night and day…

And she had an excuse for taking the ring.

If it ever came to that.

* * *

After wrapping a sheet around the painting, Noel walked to the front door of the house.

He held the painting gingerly. taking one more look at the house.

He heard a crunch of gravel.

A Volkswagen pulled into the driveway, blocking his path.

He paused in front of his Volvo.

* * *

The man coming out of the house had to be Margo's husband. Funny that Page didn't remember him from the reception. Page inspected herself in the car's rear view mirror. The man coming out of the house was young... Probably just a little younger than Margo.

Good looking too, Page thought.

Good for Margo.

Page picked up the jeweler's box from the passenger's seat, snapped open the box and peeked in at the ring.

The Alexandrite was as dark as a fallen angel's eyes.

Presentable, Page thought, taking a glance in the mirror.

I look presentable.

Summoning her courage, she leaned out the VW window and waved at Margo's husband.

He *is* young, Page thought. Page hadn't expected a doddering, old man, but Margo's husband might not even be out of school.

The man gave Page a quick look.

"Sorry I'm blocking you," Page said. "Is Margo here?"

"She's not," the man said. "Sorry."

"Can you do me a favor?"

The man shook his head. "I'm leaving now."

"You don't know when she'll be back? I had something I wanted her to appraise."

Page hated to waste the trip. She couldn't

imagine when she would summon the courage to come again.

"Can you do it for me?"

The man shrugged.

"She should be back soon," he said. "You can leave it, if you want."

He got into the car and slammed the door.

Page shifted the car into reverse and eased out of the driveway. No sound disturbed the narrow street except the Volvo's engine and the noise it's wheels made, spitting out gravel from the driveway.

Page parked by the mailbox, got out and walked into the walled courtyard from which the man had come. What should she do? Margo's husband had said that she would be right back. Page opened the box again. The ring glittered in the dim lights of the courtyard.

Could jewelry really trap a person's energy?

Where had she heard that? Page snapped the box's lid.

She would write Margo a note.

It was the only sensible thing to do. Margo was her friend.

She might be, Page realized, the only real friend that Page had in the world.

You can count on your friends, Page thought.

Going back to the car, Page took another drink, and dug through the cluttered glove compartment. She found a pen and a card from the gallery.

She was still in control. In fact, she felt better than ever.

Complete and utter perfection.

Page carefully printed the note on the back of one of the cards, crossed out Walker's name and wrote her own. She wedged it into the front door of Margo's house. She was pleased with the job. Penmanship had always been one of her talents.

She would call Margo when she got home.

Of course, Page thought, she probably wouldn't have to do that. Being such a good friend, Margo would call Page as soon as she found the note.

Of course she would.

Page knew that she would get a call from Margo by morning.

Awkwardly, Page clutched the little velvet covered box.

What if it had been a horrible mistake to take it?

What if the story Walker told Page had only been a cover? What if Tallie knew all along Page took the ring?

Page would be better off dead.

But, Page reassured herself, Tallie would never know that Page had taken the ring.

Page looked around the entryway. A ceramic frog guarded a fountain. She pulled the Day Gallery note back from the door, held the pen steady for the revision:

Margo
Sorry I missed you.

The ring's under the frog. I'll give you a call.
Page Day.

She could have written so much more, she thought.

She could have told Margo the whole story of her whole miserable life.

But what would that have proven?

And the card wasn't big enough for a memoir.

❋ ❋ ❋

The lights of Speedway were beautiful at night, Page thought. So… seasonal.

Red lights.

Green light.

Red light.

Cars honked, passing Page.

She had warm feelings for the whole world.

There was no reason for Page to hurry back into her little prison.

No reason in the whole wide world.

❋ ❋ ❋

Noel's mind raced.

The woman had seen him.

How could that have happened?

She had gotten a clear view of him, even heard his voice. Noel had no doubt that the woman would be able to identify him.

He flexed his hands on the Volvo's steering wheel.

What else could he have done?

He felt nauseated.

He should go back and assess the damages. Maybe follow the woman, see where she lives.

He hated this.

Why hadn't he listened to Fenton?

Get in and out. That had been his strategy forever. Now, everything had fallen apart.

He turned at a cul-de-sac and drove back up the hill toward the house. A rabbit skittered across the road, and Noel narrowly missed hitting it.

Could it have been five minutes since he left?

He was out of luck.

The Volkswagen was gone.

Noel got out of the car, glancing over his shoulder at the painting in the back seat.

In a quiet neighborhood like this, Noel thought, there was probably very little crime. He looked at the low hanging mesquite trees by the side of the road. He wouldn't mind living up here himself.

He glanced in the front window. The man still sprawled on the recliner.

A card poked out from the side of the front door. It hadn't been there when he left, Noel thought.

The woman left it.

The woman's name was on the card.

Page Day - The Maxwell Day Gallery

Noel smiled. He looked around the entryway.

The frog sat next to the fountain. Noel leaned over and turned it over.

He held the jewelry box, snapping it open with his thumb. The gem was a dull color in the dark light of the patio. Noel squinted. The type of stone was unfamiliar, but it was huge.

It looked valuable.

Why else would the woman have bothered leaving it for appraisal?

Noel closed the lid on the ring and slipped it into his pocket.

* * *

Jeremy woke up briefly. He was still in the recliner, but it was less comfortable than it had been.

He reached behind the chair for the bottle and took another drink.

It was dark in the room.

He took the bottle and went to bed.

* * *

The leather chairs near the bar at the Western Way were comfortable.

Page put her leg on the side of the chair and looked at the massive black window.

She was still in control. Taking a drink hadn't hurt her a bit. She knew what she was doing and she was enjoying herself for the first time in over a year.

In fact, she couldn't remember when she had felt so relaxed.

During her year off from drinking, Page realized, she had been on edge.

She realized that now.

She tested the top of the martini with her finger. A very elegant glass, she thought. Walker made too much of her drinking.

Well, she had the answer now. She would moderate her drinking. Like she was doing tonight.

Tonight she wouldn't drink so much, so fast.

She could provide a service for others, by showing that it could be done.

Total abstinence was unreasonable, Page thought.

Maybe it was a good idea for people with real problems, but not for her.

The bartender brought her a napkin and some peanuts.

He wiped the bar in front of Page.

What the hell was this?

Had she spilled something?

The bartender had to be ten years younger than her.

Very cute.

Dark curly hair.

Had he winked when he brought the napkin?

Page thought so and it pleased her.

His hair reminded her of Margo, who had the same type of hair.

Margo's hair was much longer, of course.

Margo was also very good looking. She and the bartender could have been brother and sister. It was pleasant having such good friends.

Of course, she hadn't known Margo for all that long, and she hardly knew the bartender at all.

She wondered if Margo had looked at the ring yet. How long had it been? She had been drifting along in a pleasant haze, and she hadn't paid the slightest attention to the time.

"What's your name," she said.

The bartender smiled.

"Tony."

"What time is it, Tony?"

He looked at a very nice gold watch.

Page looked at the fine hair on his wrist.

"I've got just a little past ten."

He smiled.

"Can I get you anything else?"

"It's Page," she said. "I might as well. I have a call to make, though."

Tony nodded.

"I'm making a point to pace myself," she said, pointing at the glass.

She stopped herself. She didn't need to tell Tony anything.

It might be better not to tell him anything at all.

"Always wise," Tony said, moving to the end of the bar.

Now just what the hell did he mean by that?

Was Tony commenting on her drinking?

What did he know?

She was still in control, despite the spill, which really was nothing.

She would leave this dump.

To total hell with it.

She needed to call Margo.

She slapped a bill on the bar.

"Keep the rest," she said.

She felt very virtuous by rewarding Tony.

In *spite* of his remark.

It was the right thing to do though, Page decided.

She would not let Tony, or anyone else, bring her down.

That would ruin everything.

❅ ❅ ❅

Page let the telephone ring twenty or thirty times before she realized that she had dialed Margo's number at the shop.

She had to look at the white pages to find Margo's home phone number.

She dialed the second number and let it ring. No answer.

Well, where the hell was Margo? She should have been home by now.

She carefully put the phone's receiver back and walked through the Western Way lobby.

Page started the Volkswagen and looked out over Tucson's skyline.

The blurring lights were a galaxy.

She could make it to Margo's house very easily. She really hadn't had very much to drink. Not very much at all. And she was still resolved to keep it that way. It might not be a bad idea to pick up something on the way to Margo's house.

Arriving at a person's house empty handed was very poor form.

What would Tallie say?

Page giggled.

If nothing else, she admired Tallie's sense of form.

She thought she remembered where Margo lived. If worse came to worst, the directions were somewhere in the car, but she didn't want to dig around for them.

What should she take to Margo's house?

"Chez Margo," she said aloud.

She giggled.

Her accent sounded terribly convincing.

She uttered a string of French words, not

entirely sure if the phrase meant anything.

She could feel her way to Margo's.

She would use her intuition.

Fortunately, she had plenty of that.

What to take?

The answer was obvious.

What could be more festive than a bottle of champagne?

Un magnum?

Was that big enough?

Certainement.

＊ ＊ ＊

Nobody answered Page's knock, and so she knocked harder.

It was Margo's house, Page was sure of that. For one thing, there was the ceramic frog. A remarkable work, Page thought.

She needed a frog like that. She would find one for herself... and one for Tallie, she decided in a burst of generosity.

She peeked under the frog.

Obviously, Margo had taken the ring.

Would Margo ever have seen such a splendid gem?

In a way, Page felt sorry for Margo.

Page's new friend didn't seem to have the happiest of lives.

She slapped her forehead. There was a doorbell, right in front of her. How silly could she be?

She rang the doorbell.

Again.

Again.

No answer.

She walked into the unlocked house.

Might as well be comfortable, she thought.

Nobody here but us chickens.

It was very dark. Probably Margo and her handsome husband would be home soon.

In the meantime, Page felt tired. She thought she would take a nap.

Just a quick one, of course.

A catnap. She didn't want to miss anything.

The night was young.

She found a bed, put down the bottle of champagne and stretched out.

She had opened the champagne, but was willing to share.

Only a catnap, she reminded herself. She felt a draft. Someone had left a window open. Page clutched the sheets.

Soft flannel.

Goldilocks without the rigmarole.

This one was *just* right.

She would only stay a minute, she thought, closing her eyes.

❖ ❖ ❖

Margo drove home.

She snapped on the lights in the living room. The painting was gone.

Thank God for Fenton's friend, Margo thought.

Jeremy must have managed to get to bed.

She went into the bedroom.

The lights were off and it was hard to see.

Margo saw enough, though.

The woman in bed with Jeremy was sound asleep.

This was new.

A new low for Jeremy.

She couldn't say that she was terribly surprised.

But this was the last straw.

She decided to spend the night at the shop.

✳ ✳ ✳

Noel looked at the ring under the Volvo's interior light. How would Fenton react to the ring?

Fenton couldn't object. No way in the world.

Noel remembered distinctly Fenton's instructions.

All right, so Noel had followed them.

Besides the painting, there hadn't been anything else worth taking.

But the ring was different.

And the ring hadn't been *in* the house.

Noel opened the top of the box again. The diamonds surrounding the purplish gem were by themselves magnificent.

Noel still hadn't decided whether he would show the ring to Fenton. Fenton couldn't object to the ring, could he?

On one hand, Fenton could lose his temper and pay Noel less for the painting.

That would be a shame.

On the other hand, if the ring was as valuable as it looked, Fenton might want first shot at buying it.

The woman who left the ring said something about an appraisal. She thought that he lived there. Maybe the guy passed out in the recliner did that kind of work.

Noel shrugged his shoulders. It didn't make any difference either way.

He was tempted to go directly to Fenton's house and wake the old man up. He pictured Fenton asleep in his bed.

Just like Scrooge, stocking cap and all.

Fenton, however, had been very specific. Noel was to bring the painting at the appointed hour tomorrow morning.

No sooner.

It didn't pay to do things your own way when you were dealing with Matthew Fenton.

Noel worked the Volvo over the railroad tracks and through downtown. He would be home way before schedule.

He had a bad thought. What if Ed was waiting

for him?

It would be just like Ed. He didn't seem to have anything better to do.

And he sure as hell couldn't let Ed see the painting. The thing might end up with a hole in the middle if Ed went into his Mike Hammer routine.

He would just have to be careful and scout the place before parking.

Ed's big gold Trans-Am was easy to spot.

He circled the block. Most of the houses on his street had luminarias out. There were still a few houses without them, but the warm lights gave a nice overall impression.

He decided that if everything went well with Fenton, he would put out luminarias himself.

Everything looked safe, but just to be sure, Noel pulled the emergency brake a block from his house.

No use announcing to Ed that he was home.

Noel considered whether or not he should go out again. He snapped the lights on in the bungalow and put the covered painting on a chair. He felt his pocket to make sure the ring was still there.

So far, so good.

Maybe he would go out again.

This might be a good night.

It had been good so far.

Noel stood next to the painting and lifted the frame slightly up from the chair, pulling the sheet out from under.

Slowly, he took the sheet off, savoring every moment of the disrobing.

Noel shook his head.

What was it about the painting? He almost believed the thing was bewitched.

Something was very familiar about the two figures in the painting.

Noel was hungry again. He took the saucepan from the stove and swished the leftover noodles out with a plastic spatula. He ran tap water into the bottom and turned on the gas jets.

He would make rice.

Hominy and rice.

He promised himself that even before he brought Gladys the rent, he would treat himself to a steak dinner.

He could almost hear the sizzle now.

What the hell, Noel thought. It was a good night. He would go out again. Take the car to a new area.

Somewhere he'd never worked. See what he could rustle up.

What about Ed? Ed had broken in before. How else would he have known about Noel's jewelry collection? It wouldn't be a good idea to leave the painting around. Fenton would never give him another job if he messed this up.

The painting fit nicely behind the refrigerator. Noel covered it with two days worth of newspaper.

He noticed the sports section headline:

Cats Win Big.

* * *

Noel turned off the lights in the kitchen. He tapped his pocket. The ring was still in the box safely tucked in his pocket. He would keep it with him for good luck.

He glanced at his watch. Almost time to head out.

He opened the medicine cabinet in his bathroom. Swinging the mirror away from himself he saw his profile in the mirror in front of the claw foot tub he had painted gold last summer.

He took a cotton ball from a bag.

He opened a lid of the zinc oxide and sniffed it.

Slowly and deliberately he started to apply the white grease to his face.

THE STEADY BEAT OF HIS PULSE

Jeremy awoke Thursday morning, with a dry mouth and an unusually low sense of self-esteem.

He was in bed. During the night, he must have moved from the recliner. He pulled his blanket tightly around his shoulders.

He looked at the woman next to him in bed.

God, he thought, Margo.

How long would she put up with him?

She was covered by one of the flannel sheets, and all that he could hear was her rhythmic breathing.

Margo must have put him to bed, he thought.

He took the blanket from the end of the bed and covered her more thoroughly.

He looked at his watch.

He had been out like a light for how many hours?

He couldn't remember seeing or hearing Margo come in.

Thinking about his wife made Jeremy feel guilty.

Why did he keep putting her through these things?

He needed coffee.

Shower first, then coffee.

And Margo thought he couldn't take care of himself. He would be fine later in the day.

Later in the day? That was a joke. The day was well underway, and Margo would usually be at the store by this time, waiting for customers who never arrived. Should he go down to the store and open for her?

Let her get a little more sleep?

Maybe he would do that more willingly if Margo didn't blame him for everything.

What had happened?

Jeremy took the cold coffee from the machine and poured a cup into a saucepan. He would have to think very carefully about it. Something had happened. It was like a dream.

Something happened, Jeremy thought.

He couldn't remember a thing. His mind felt like mush.

Then he remembered the painting.

Oh God, Jeremy thought. It wasn't a dream. Forgetting about the coffee, Jeremy ran toward the living room, slamming his shin against the leg of a chair.

His head reeled. Jeremy had to sit on the kitchen floor and hold his leg.

The pain was intense.

The painting. He remembered now.

He crept forward on the tiles, putting his hands on the floor and pushing himself upward. He limped back into the living room.

There was no painting on the chair.

Jeremy slumped on the recliner, holding his head in one hand and his damaged leg with the other.

Was he going nuts?

It was so vivid. Jeremy pictured the way the painting had looked as if it had really been there.

It had to be a dream.

* * *

Jeremy felt the steady beat of his pulse underneath his temple. How could something so real have only been a dream?

The more he thought about it, the more confused Jeremy became. He remembered the painting now. It was a Maxwell Day. He was absolutely sure of it. Just like the ones he and Margo saw at the Day Gallery.

For all he knew, the gallery was where he saw the painting. Displayed nicely, no doubt, under track lighting. Just part of the display.

That would make the dream reasonable, anyway.

It had to be a combination of wishful thinking and a very vivid dream.

He had to get to the car. He hoped there was gas in the thing. Jeremy could only generally remember the gallery's location. Margo had driven there. He picked up the yellow pages and thumbed through until he found the address.

The gallery was miles away on the east side of town.

* * *

Walker Day's habit was to personally greet the first person to walk into the gallery every morning. He knew that he had seen this man before. He recognized the man, despite the unkempt hair and a two day growth of beard.

An artist?

"Good morning," Walker said. Walker tried his best to be pleasant, but it was a hard feat.

Page had disappeared. Walker couldn't decide if he should call the police, or wait for her to come home on her own. He knew that he would decide to wait. He always did.

Passivity was his nature.

The police wouldn't be interested in his concerns about Page.

Only if she was dead.

That was a chilling thought.

Page could be dead.

Obviously she had started drinking again.

"I'm fascinated by these paintings."

The man wore rimless glasses over red eyes.

Walker remembered. The man had been a guest at the reception the other night. He had spent most of his time at the canapé table.

He wasn't wearing a nametag now. Presumably he had been an invited guest. Tallie would remember his name.

"Nice to see you again," Walker said, extending a hand. "Walker Day."

"An honor," the man said. "I'm Jeremy Powers. I didn't get a chance to talk with you the other night."

"No," Walker said.

"I just had to come back and look again. That's all right, isn't it?"

Walker smiled. "Of course. Make yourself at home."

❋ ❋ ❋

The painting had been a Maxwell Day. There was no doubt about that. Looking at the paintings again, Jeremy was certain.

Other examples of Day's work shared similarities to what he now thought of as the dream painting.

Jeremy paused in front of a nude, reclining on a chaise, her face turned slightly away from the artist.

An odalisque.

The woman looked familiar.

"How wonderful to see you again, Jeremy."

The woman smiled at him. Tallie Day. The owner of the gallery. He remembered her from the reception. Quick footwork had saved him from disaster. She turned out to be a good sport. She had a sense of humor.

Jeremy laughed. "Good morning Mrs. Day. I couldn't resist coming back."

"We like that," she said. "In fact, we depend on that, as I'm sure that you and your charming wife do."

"Absolutely," Jeremy said. "Margo really enjoyed herself. I can't say when we've had as good a time."

Tallie smiled. "I'm glad to hear that. Come any time."

Jeremy tried not to stare.

The nude may have been painted at least forty years before, but Tallie was still recognizable.

"I was wondering about a particular painting."

Tallie looked quizzically at him. "One of Maxwell's?"

"Yes," Jeremy said. He needed to be careful. "It's one that I saw somewhere." He looked around the room. "I thought it was here, but I guess…"

"What did it look like?"

Tallie came closer to Jeremy.

He detected a trace of the woman's perfume.

"Oh, I'm sure you know the painting," Jeremy said, pointing to a painting across from the nude. "It's about this size. Interesting choice of subjects though. I'm not an expert in your husband's work, but I wondered if it's the only one he did with this particular subject. An officer…"

Tallie stared at him.

"A cavalry officer, I should say," Jeremy added.

Tallie closed her eyes slightly. "Anything else?

"He's sitting in front of a campfire with an Indian."

"An officer and an Indian, you say."

"Exactly." Jeremy said. "That's it exactly."

Tallie looked over her shoulder. Walker was at the other end of the gallery.

"I'm sorry Mr. Powers," she said, flashing a smile. "I'm afraid that wouldn't be one of Maxwell's paintings."

❉ ❉ ❉

Noel slept later than usual.

After a shower, he put the painting in the back of the Volvo.

He checked his watch. He still had plenty of time.

Noel needed to put some gas in the car. The show of generosity to the waitress yesterday set Noel back, and he hadn't made much last night. He pulled some crumpled bills from his pocket. All ones. Some change, too, but not very much.

Three dollars worth of gas would get him to Fenton's house.

He could fill the tank when he left.

❈ ❈ ❈

Fenton's reaction to the painting was odd. He watched as Noel pulled off one layer after another of the Tucson newspaper.

Fenton stood back, shook his head.

"I never thought I'd see this again," he said.

Noel did not answer.

Fenton shrugged. "It's the real thing, all right."

Noel cleared his throat. "You've seen it before?"

Fenton nodded. "I watched it being painted. I was there."

Unbelievable, Noel thought.

No wonder Fenton was so insistent upon getting hold of the painting.

Fenton pulled out a gold money clip from his wallet. Indifferently, he tossed the clip and the wad of bills toward Noel. "I know we agreed upon a price."

Noel grabbed the clip. Looked at it.

"That ought to hold you," Fenton said.

Noel was pleased. He tried to not make it obvious as he thumbed through the bills. Fenton had gone over by about twenty percent.

It was enough to make him lose his sense of caution.

Figuring that Fenton was in a celebratory mood,

Noel took out the box from his pocket, and showed Fenton the ring.

The Alexandrite sparkled in the light of Fenton's living room.

"What's that supposed to be?" Fenton said. He eyed Noel suspiciously. "You didn't take that from her…" Fenton stopped. "You didn't take that from the same house, did you?"

"Absolutely not," Noel said. "I thought you might be able to tell me something about this."

"So, you didn't answer. What's this supposed to be, a mood ring?"

Noel's jaw tightened. "Why don't you take a look for yourself?"

Fenton dug around in a crowded desk drawer. He pulled out a loupe. He didn't spend a second examining the ring.

Using his thumb and middle fingers, Fenton flipped the ring back to Noel.

"I see you still got bullshit taste," he laughed. "You must have picked this up at the street fair. It might be worth fifteen bucks."

"Bullshit," Noel said.

Fenton smiled. "No, but it's close."

✳   ✳   ✳

Noel went straight to the gas station and filled the Volvo with high test. Slipped a hundred in the slot and waited while the guy went through the magic marker routine. Noel could have told the guy not to worry. Fenton wouldn't pay him with counterfeit bills.

There was a lot of change from the hundred. With the rest of the cash it made for a good payday.

He was set for a while.

After paying off Gladys, who could say what he would do with the rest of the loot?

He slapped the side of his pocket.

Fenton thought the ring was a fake?

Noel knew better than that.

✻ ✻ ✻

Fenton thought about the painting.

He remembered the day Max unveiled it. Max was a quick one. How long had it taken him to finish the thing?

It was a masterpiece – Fenton had recognized that at first glance. The fact that Max called it 'The Truce' was significant.

It was painful for Fenton to think of that day.

Max had included the ring in the painting.

If you looked closely enough at the painting, you could see the ring in the hand of the cavalry officer.

The ring Max had given to Tallie when he found out she was pregnant.

The ring.

Fenton felt sick.

LEPRECHAUNS

A violent noise came from the clock radio and a wrecking ball in Page's head swung forward with nauseating intensity. If she could go back to sleep, Page thought, she might not hurt so badly.

She stayed in bed, keeping her eyes slightly closed, knowing that she would have to get up eventually.

She knew from experience that she would not die.

She badly needed a drink.

It wasn't her worst hangover ever, but it was her most recent.

She had been free of this hell for a year.

Why had she done it?

She fixed her eyes on the dark ceiling of the room and pulled the blanket up to her chin.

Was it the air conditioner blasting arctic air that made her scalp hurt?

No, she thought, it was just cold.

It didn't look like a motel room.

Thank God for that, Page thought.

A Frida Kahlo print swam along on the wall.

Page's stomach lurched.

No sudden moves, she thought. A gyroscope whirred smoothly at the top of her head, maintaining a delicate balance. Page knew that if she tilted her head, the gyroscope would clatter out of control and the wrecking ball would swing forward again.

If she could keep the gyroscope stable, she would be fine.

She breathed in.

Out.

Success.

At this rate, she would be herself in a couple of years.

A drink, she thought... even a small one, would make this go away.

"Meredith."

She whispered her sister's name.

Page knew that she would have to call her.

What would Meredith say?

Oh Christ, Page thought. What have I done?

It took concentration for Page to creep out of the bed. She braced her hand against the carpet and worked her legs toward the side of the bed. The Saltillo tiles were freezing. She couldn't afford any sudden movement of her head.

Upset the gyroscope and the wrecking ball would swing.

And the pain would come back worse than before.

The numbers on the clock radio flipped over.

Page worked her way out of the bed and into the

bathroom.

The high intensity bathroom lights shocked her system. She crept along the cold tiles. She couldn't face the sight in the mirror.

She wondered if she should try calling Meredith.

She would call her later, she decided.

She would have to call eventually, but she couldn't bear the idea of hearing her sister's concerned voice right now.

Page huddled near the toilet bowl.

Three leprechauns sang out of key in her head.

Why wouldn't they stop?

She leaned over and propped her chin against the toilet seat.

The leprechauns chattered excitedly.

She had slept in her clothes.

At least she knew where they were. Page supposed she should be grateful.

After vomiting, Page turned on the shower to a pulse setting. She lay on the shower floor, letting the hot water pound her body.

If she could find a drink and a telephone, she would be all right.

She was in somebody's house.

Just like Goldilocks.

Page, pushing through the yogurt and milk in the refrigerator, found a can of tomato juice and two cans of beer.

Her hands shook as she poured the two together into a glass.

Sitting cross legged on the throw rug in the

living room, she held the glass with both hands and moved it to her dry lips.

It did Page a world of good.

She looked around the place.

How had she stumbled in here?

The living room was totally unfamiliar.

She took another sip.

My God, she thought, I may just get to be human again.

A phone lay on the table next to an orange recliner. What time was it? The heavy curtains in the room were keeping out the sun. The wrecking ball was gradually getting smaller.

But *she* was still a wreck.

She tried reconstructing the events that brought her here.

She remembered going into the liquor store, and the lights on Speedway.

And then nothing. Nothing until waking up here. Page felt the ridges on the recliner and looked at the telephone.

A newspaper lay beside the chair.

Cats Win Big.

At least she was still in Tucson.

Something else bothered her. What was it? Page worked at the corners of the problem, trying to remember.

With a sickening lurch she stood up, pulled open the curtains, and felt the intensely bright mid-morning sun.

She was on a residential street.

Goldilocks.

Who could say when the three bears would return?

She felt inside her purse, looking for her dark glasses.

She would need another drink soon, and as Walker would have said, she was presently cash poor.

She put the extra can of beer in her purse.

To hell with Walker anyway, she thought.

She reached for the phone.

Maybe Meredith would be decent enough to give her a ride home.

Oh, God, she thought.

The ring.

Margo.

She pulled the can of beer from her bag.

One tiny more drink, and she might even be able to figure things out.

THE RUBY
GRAPEFRUIT

Today she would finish her Christmas shopping, Meredith O'Toole promised herself.

Finish?

Hardly.

Today she would start her Christmas shopping.

The yearly routine was less of an ordeal this year than it had been than last. She was spending less time wondering what Rob was doing for Christmas.

She was certain that her ex-husband was having a fine time. With Camille, of course. Wasn't that the girl's name?

All Meredith really wanted to do during the semester break was to relax. But that was out of the question.

She spooned out the last section of the ruby grapefruit, and squeezed the juice into a saucer. Meredith looked out the plate glass window onto the patio where birds gathered daily on the feeder.

Another beautiful day.

I'm lucky, Meredith thought.

I'm a survivor.

The phone rang.

Meredith looked at the grapefruit rind. She wondered if it was something that birds would enjoy. Normally she put them on the compost heap. Maybe the birds would like them.

She picked up the phone.

Page.

Crying.

"Slow down, baby," Meredith said.

So much for shopping.

RELATIVE DEXTERITY

Gladys was grateful for the money. Grateful and a little surprised. She counted the hundreds in front of Noel.

"You're good for another month," she said.

"Merry Christmas," Noel said. He was still standing in front of her house. "Your lights look nice."

Gladys shook her head. "Don't let yourself get so far behind again," she said. "You're a nice young man."

"I won't," Noel said.

As far as he knew, he was telling the truth. He certainly would try not to be late on the rent.

"Ed will be pleased you made good on this."

Noel nodded. Ed might or might not be happy about it.

Ed might just as easily be irritated he wouldn't have any reason to come over and play bad cop.

* * *

Ed knocked on Noel's door. Noel looked out the window, hoping Gladys was with Ed. Anything to temper him.

No such luck. Ed was by himself, red-faced, blowing on his hands to keep them warm.

It was unusual how cold the last couple of days had turned out, Noel thought. He really needed his jacket when he went out at night.

Noel looked back out the window. Ed stood, shifting from one foot to another.

He looked impatient.

Cold and impatient.

Noel could delay things by cutting out the back, jumping in the car and taking off for a while.

That wouldn't resolve anything with Ed, though. A guy like Ed would keep coming back if Noel showed any weakness.

What the hell, Noel thought.

He didn't owe Gladys anything, so he didn't need to worry about Ed.

Cautiously, Noel opened the door.

Slightly.

Ed didn't look angry. Noel opened the door.

Ed squinted at Noel. "You paid your rent."

Noel nodded. "An extra month even. Did Gladys tell you that?"

"That's good," Ed said. "Your ship must have

come in."

"Can I do something for you?" Noel shut the door slightly in an effort to keep out the cold air.

Ed nudged his shoulder inside the door.

Might as well let him in, Noel thought, releasing his grip on the door.

Ed plunged inside.

"We gotta talk," Ed said.

"I'm listening."

"You must not have been listening very carefully the other night," Ed took a few steps toward the covered card table.

Noel stepped with him, attempting to keep his own body between Ed and the table. Maybe Ed had already seen the stuff, but there was no reason to get another look. Particularly not since Noel had put the ring in the case with the other jewelry.

It was no use. Ed was on a mission.

He looked at Noel.

"You know, buddy, I've spent a lot of years dealing with guys like you."

Clearly, Ed didn't intend for Noel to answer.

Ed pushed his way past Noel and stood next to the card table, fingering the hem of the tablecloth.

"Almost a lifetime," Ed added. "Guys just like you. A few women, too."

He picked up the edge of the cloth, teasing it back from the jewelry case. "I always managed to find a way to get along, though."

He grinned at Noel. "You know why?"

Noel shrugged. The cloth was almost completely

off the case.

"That's all right," Ed said. "Don't strain yourself. I'll just go ahead and tell you why."

With a quick snapping motion, Ed pulled the cloth completely away.

What a dope, Noel thought.

Ed thought that trick was impressive?

Noel could pull a cloth out from under a fully set dinner table, leaving full glasses of water undisturbed. Noel doubted that Ed had that kind of manual dexterity.

Ed's stunt was relative child's play.

"You know why I get along?" Ed said. "I never discourage creativity."

What the hell was Ed talking about? Noel watched as Ed felt along the side of the jewelry case for the latch.

Ed looked up from the case at Noel.

"I don't want to discourage your natural talent."

Ed was trying for a nasty-nice demeanor, and falling short.

"I know guys like you. You're like tigers. You never lose your spots."

"Leopards," Noel said.

"Whatever," Ed said. "I know you. I've been watching you."

Ed opened the case and made a mock display of surprise at the contents.

"Look at what we got here," he said, rifling his hands through the jewelry. "You robbed Liberace?"

"It's costume jewelry," Noel said. "None of it's

very valuable."

Ed shook his head. "That's a shame." Ed dropped the lid back on the case. "I was going to propose an arrangement."

Noel hoped Ed didn't notice he was holding his breath.

"An arrangement," Ed said. "You got a talent as a break-in artist." He held up his hand. "Now don't deny it. It's true. Like I said, I've been in this business since you were in juvie."

"Listen," Noel said, "you can't just come in here and..."

Ed turned to face Noel.

"That's enough,' he growled. "I told you, I got an arrangement. It's worked for how long, I don't even know."

He stopped. He wanted to make sure that Noel was taking it all in.

"You go ahead and keep on doing what you're doing. And all I'm going to do is take a little something now and again. You stay in line, and I won't get greedy."

Ed opened the lid again.

Shit, Noel thought.

Not the ring. Please not the ring.

"I been looking for something for a lady," Ed said. "Something nice." He paused, looking over the jewelry as if deciding on a piece of chocolate.

"None of it's worth anything," Noel said. "You're wasting your time."

Ed looked up.

"Then maybe you better get better stuff."

He picked up a bracelet.

"This is nice," Ed said. "Kinda classy... She might like it."

Go ahead, Noel thought.

Just not the ring.

The ring was in the corner of the box. With any luck, Ed wouldn't notice it.

"Oh, hell no," Ed said.

He reached again and pulled up the ring.

The Alexandrite twinkled purplish gray.

"Now that's nice," Ed said. "That's something you don't see every day."

MEREDITH IN PROFILE

The setting sun streaked orange across the western sky. Trinity was heading home feeling relaxed and clear-headed. He always felt that way an hour into one of his runs. Forty minutes had passed since his body stopped its inevitable protests. He loved winter in Tucson. Earlier, he had dug around for something warm and put on a hooded gray sweatshirt. The evening run usually took Trinity from the Presidio neighborhood up to 4th Avenue. After crossing the railroad tracks, Trinity would wind his way back through the underpass and then downtown. Tonight, ambition and the pure pleasure of the run took Trinity past University Boulevard all the way to Speedway before his return.

A woman stood in profile next to the bougainvillea Trinity had planted next to his adobe. The sky was too dark for Trinity to be certain, but the woman could be Meredith O'Toole.

He had left the lights off before his run. Shadow from a solitary street lamp fell across the porch and the woman's outline.

Even the thought of Meredith quickened his pulse. Reaching the walkway in front of his house, Trinity put his hands to his waist and slowed to a walk.

Trinity smelled Meredith's perfume in the cool evening air. They could have both been eighteen again, standing in line together in front of Bear Down Gym waiting to sign up for classes.

Time does funny things, Trinity thought. He remembered his feelings on the first night they kissed. It was almost as if twenty years hadn't passed.

"How are you, Frank?" she said.

Her voice still husky and dark; her dark eyes passionate.

He held the porch rail.

She waited for him.

"I'm fine, Meredith... I need some water."

What brought her to his house? The few times Trinity had seen her since he got out of the army she had been friendly but distant... as though afraid of old feelings being resurrected.

She took the time to find out where I live, Trinity thought, and the first thing I manage to say is that I need water.

Trinity kept the letter she sent to him all the way through basic training.

Dear Frank... the letter started.

He glanced at her hand. No wedding ring.

"It's good to see you, Meredith. "

"Oh, Frank." Meredith smiled. "You better get your water. I'll take some too."

Thank God the kitchen's clean, he thought, snapping on the light in the front room.

He filled two tumblers with ice water from the earthenware crock he kept chilled in the refrigerator. He sprayed a stream of water over the top of the dishes in the sink. At least make them look semi-clean, he thought.

Meredith peered over the top of the glass at Trinity.

"It's my sister, Frank. You remember Page, don't you?"

Trinity vaguely remembered a younger sister.

He sipped the water. Meredith's manner wasn't natural. She was forcing an artificial ebullience.

"Your younger sister, right? By quite a few years..."

Trinity put the glass down.

"Sorry," he said. "A few years. She wore braces, I think."

Meredith sighed.

"That was Page. But she's all grown up now."

Meredith's profile made a dim silhouette against the whitewashed wall of the kitchen.

It has to be trouble, he thought.

She's not even sure she wants to be here.

"Page has a big problem," Meredith said. "I hope you can help."

"Try me," Trinity said.

As if Trinity wouldn't do anything for her.

Meredith's face was serious.

"Page should have the most ideal life you can imagine. She has everything. Everything she could want. Married to a great guy... Frank, I can't believe any of this."

Meredith shivered. She was on the verge of tears.

Trinity stood next to Meredith and put his arm around her shoulder.

Seeing Meredith in this setting seemed unreal. Only the real life sounds of the street kept it from being a dream.

"Tell me about it."

"She's my little sister," she said, "I still remember baking cookies with her."

Meredith laughed, and then her voice broke.

"I'm so scared."

Trinity led Meredith into the living room and cleared the pile of newspapers and magazines from the leather armchair.

He stepped away from her.

Meredith held the water glass. She was trying to keep from crying.

"That's all right," Trinity said, "go ahead and cry."

"I can't," she said. "If I start, I might not stop."

"It's all right," Trinity said. "Start at the beginning."

"Can I ask a huge favor of you?" Meredith said, managing a brief smile. "Would you mind making some coffee? She's in a hell of a mess."

"I can manage the coffee," Trinity said.

It was a good night for coffee.

The run had made him feel relaxed.

He could have used a shower, though.

"What's this about a mess? You're talking about right now?" Trinity looked around the kitchen. Somewhere in this house, he had to have a box of tissues. He poured a carafe of water into the coffee maker.

From the kitchen doorway, Trinity saw Meredith look up. Starting to recover, she looked around the room, taking in everything from the mesquite ribs of the high ceiling to the chipped blue paint on the door.

From Trinity's vintage baseball bats to the small collection of bola ties hanging on the wall.

What would she think about the piles of books on the cinder block shelves?

Early Value Village.

Home sweet home, Trinity thought.

He dumped a couple of scoops of Ethiopian coffee into the coffee maker.

Haile Selassie, he thought.

He tossed in two more.

Might as well make it very Haile Selassie.

Trinity called in to Meredith. "Does she live here in town?"

The coffee maker began to make its creature-from-the-deep noises.

Great timing, Trinity thought.

On top of not having any tissue to offer, the coffee maker needs an exorcism.

He really needed to replace the damned thing.

And buy tissues.

He couldn't remember the last time he brewed coffee at night. Mornings, Trinity usually skipped the coffee making ordeal and grabbed a cup from the Presidio Market.

Lesley brewed better coffee anyway.

"Up past Sunrise," Meredith said. "She's lived there since she and Walker got married. That's been years."

The coffee maker's obscure groans could be heard in the living room.

Meredith knitted her brow. "Does that thing work?"

Trinity took the pot from the machine and poured a small shot of the coffee into a china teacup. He held the cup back under the drizzle to fill it.

"Damn straight, it works." Trinity, said, sliding the pot back into its slot. "This baby could bring down the Berlin Wall."

He put a saucer under the cup before taking it into the living room and giving it to Meredith.

"I can't remember how much younger Page is," he said. "Time does funny things, doesn't it?"

He waited. "Do you want anything in that?"

He might have something here, somewhere.

Meredith sipped the coffee then shook her head. "It's fine..."

She held the cup and saucer and looked at Trinity.

"Page is actually just four years younger than I am." Her lips left a scarlet smudge on the rim's gold band. "You do the math."

Trinity walked back into the kitchen and pulled another cup and saucer from the cupboard. The machine sputtered and the coffee spilled on the heating element, causing a hiss.

Some people ran vinegar through these things, Trinity thought. He'd tried it once. It made the house smell like boiled cabbage, and it didn't fix the coffee maker.

Better to throw the thing out.

It didn't owe him a dime.

Returning to the living room, Trinity stared over the top of his cup at Meredith. "Okay, I did the math."

Meredith looked at him, smiled, and gently shook her head.

"Page is fragile," she said. "I don't know any better way to put it. She's always been vulnerable. I thought that being married to Walker would make a difference, but it hasn't."

Trinity nodded. "Fragile... Did you say that Walker's got money?"

"I didn't, why do you ask?"

"Just a guess," Trinity said. He leaned forward. "It doesn't matter. Can you flesh out the fragile part?"

"You might as well know, Frank. Walker is Walker Day."

Meredith stopped, as if letting the information

sink in.

"He's Maxwell Day's son," she said.

"Nice gig," Trinity said.

Maxwell Day.

An artist in the tradition of Charles Russell and Frederic Remington.

All three of them would fit neatly in the same paragraph.

Trinity took a deep breath.

Being Maxwell Day's son would be nice work if you could get it.

Walker wouldn't be suffering.

"The gallery's fabulous, Frank," Meredith said. "You've been there, haven't you?"

"All the time," Trinity said. "Whenever I need to update my collection."

Meredith shook her head. "You might think that Walker's a dilettante. He's not... He's really made an effort to keep the gallery current."

"I understand all that. You're telling me that Walker's a peach. But you said something about Page being vulnerable. What's that all about?"

"Let's put it this way," Meredith said. She held her finger beneath her lower lip, "People can easily take advantage of my sister. My parents were aware of it long before I ever was."

"Were?"

"Dad died a few years ago, and my mother can barely take care of herself. The last thing I want to do is to drag her into this. In fact, I'd just as soon my mother doesn't know anything about it."

Meredith held the cup close to her forehead and closed her eyes.

Trinity sipped his coffee. It was obvious there was more to Meredith's story.

"Tell me what happened."

"It's not just what's happened, per se, Frank," she said. "It's what might happen. She's lost a piece of jewelry."

Meredith paused.

"A ring. A very valuable ring. She shouldn't have had it in the first place."

Trinity sipped the coffee. It was strong enough to float a three-penny nail.

"A ring?"

"A ring," Meredith repeated. "It's kind of like calling the Taj Mahal a summer home."

She lowered her voice.

"Frank, I can't even tell you how valuable it is. It belongs to Walker's mother."

Meredith brought the cup to her lips.

Trinity remembered the first time that he kissed Meredith. Could it have been twenty years? Longer, he thought.

"Tallie... Walker's mother doesn't know Page has the ring?"

The kiss took place next to a sprinkler on the lawn in front of Old Main. An October evening. A cool evening. Not as cold as this one.

"At this point," Meredith said, "Page can't even tell me why she took it."

They had to move when the water came on.

Trinity remembered the two of them laughing as the unexpected shower soaked their clothes.

"You talked to her?"

"A couple of hours ago," Meredith said. "But I could barely make sense of what she was saying."

Twenty years. A child born that year could be in college.

"It doesn't sound complicated," Trinity said. "How's the coffee."

Meredith took another tentative sip. "It's fine, Frank. It really speaks with authority."

"It's Ethiopian," he said. "It's probably an acquired taste. So what are we talking about here, the Hope Diamond?"

Meredith shook her head. "Frank, I'm counting on you to take this at least somewhat seriously."

"I think I understand," Trinity said. "She takes the ring from her mother-in-law's jewelry box. She's not sure why... And now she's lost it."

"It's an Alexandrite, Frank. And it's worth a fortune. Tallie should keep the thing in a safety deposit box."

"Tallie the mother-in-law..."

Meredith nodded.

"She does have a problem," Trinity said. "Actually the insurance company has a problem."

Meredith shook her head. "That's why I'm here. Page is terrified. She was raving on and on about leaving Walker. Then she told me about the ring."

"Does she get along with the old lady?"

"You mean Tallie? Tallie couldn't possibly be

nicer. An old, old family. She helps Walker run the gallery."

Meredith held up her hand.

"This is too much Frank. I don't think Page has the slightest idea what she's gotten herself into."

"If you're asking me to find the ring, I might as well be blunt. I don't know if I can help you." Trinity stood in the kitchen doorway.

The coffee maker was still making terrible groaning sounds, reminding Trinity of a subtitled Japanese war movie he had once seen. Probably one of the many films he'd seen with Meredith at the New Loft.

"I'm coming to you on business," Meredith said, "but also because I know you, Frank."

"And I'm not your run-of-the-mill detective, right?"

"That's not what I mean, Frank. I came here because I trust you." Meredith paused and looked at Trinity. "I can pay."

With all of his heart, Trinity wished that Meredith had said something else.

"Sorry, Meredith," Trinity said. "My metal detector's in the shop. It got a little banged up looking for quarters in Randolph Park."

Meredith's eyes dropped from Trinity's and she looked at her hands. "It's all right Frank. If you don't want to help, I understand."

Trinity took the cup from Meredith. She turned down the offer of a refill.

"Page called you from home?"

"No," she said. Meredith turned away from Trinity and let the word trail off.

The room became very quiet.

"Frank," Meredith said. "I should have told you this. It isn't just simply the ring that's missing. Page decided to run away from home." Meredith stopped. "That's not completely accurate," she said, "she's at my house now. I picked her up this morning."

Trinity stopped in the doorway to the kitchen. He turned back toward Meredith.

"Say that again."

Meredith's face went blank.

"Damn it," she said. "I should have told you this all in order. The ring's *missing*. Page doesn't have it, and when we had our little conversation this morning... Page kept saying over and over... Saying she couldn't get it back, and she was leaving Walker. She was practically hysterical."

Trinity squinted at Meredith. "Sorry, Meredith. You lost me. Does she have the ring, or not?"

"She left the ring at a friend's house..."

"So far, no problem," Trinity said, putting the teacup on his knee. "You want me to go get it?"

Meredith shook her head. "It's not as simple as that, Frank. There's more to it. The ring is missing." Meredith turned away from Trinity. "I should have told you. Page drinks too much when she's under stress."

Trinity nodded.

"She's not an alcoholic," Meredith said quickly.

"I'm not saying that. But when she comes back from these episodes, she can't account for herself."

"Episodes?"

Meredith nodded. "That's what they're called."

"Is she in any condition to talk tonight?"

"Tomorrow," Meredith said. "She should be sleeping now. I told her to go ahead and take something."

"Something?" Trinity said.

"I watched her take the pill, Frank. She's asleep. But I made sure that she didn't have any more lying around."

"Is your sister suicidal?"

"I wouldn't say so... I don't think so."

Meredith stood by the door.

Was she looking for an invitation to stay?

"Try to get some sleep," Trinity said. "There's no reason to worry right now."

"Trinity," Meredith said. "Frank..."

He took her hand.

"I'm glad you came here, Meredith," he said. "I'm happy to do this."

✽ ✽ ✽

After Meredith left, Trinity stood by the door and wrote a list of names on an index card.

Walker Day - Page's husband
Tallie Day - mother-in-law
Page Day - Meredith's sister

Would he have taken the job for anyone other than Meredith?

Not on a bet.

Some women drink under stress.

And Meredith's sister had absconded with the crown jewels.

A nice little job for Frank Trinity.

Trinity rolled the empty teacup idly in his hands, remembering the way Meredith's body felt against his own.

Twenty years can pass in the blink of an eye and make hardly as much difference.

Trinity felt like Rip Van Winkle. He had missed a lot during those twenty years.

So Page had grown up and had married Maxwell Day's son.

Trinity missed that wedding, just like he'd missed Meredith's.

Trinity balanced the saucer on top of his teacup.

In twenty years, Meredith never had changed her name from O'Toole.

And she didn't wear a ring.

THE CASA SOLANA SWIMMING POOL

What the hell was he doing with his life?

Ed rarely became philosophical, but recent events made him wonder.

Just because he got set up at work.

So what?

Was he going to throw everything else in his life away?

It didn't make sense.

He leaned back in the chaise. The pool at the Casa Solana was deserted, but Ed hoped that some of the women who came down here to sunbathe would keep him company.

He crossed his legs.

He felt a little self-conscious after his experience with Eileen.

He didn't want to look too much like an off-duty cop. Technically, he had never even been a cop.

Some women were just skittish.

Eileen for example.

Ed hadn't seen her since she suggested that he take a job as a bouncer at her club.

He could just feature that happening.

Ed felt the outline of the jewelry box. Why the hell had he taken the ring from that loser?

The thing obviously wasn't real.

Something that big would be worth a fortune.

Ed pulled out the box and looked at the ring. It really looked great in the sun. He snapped the box shut.

It hadn't hurt letting Noel know who was boss.

It would be a long time before the guy tried to stiff Gladys on the rent again, that much was for sure.

Meanwhile, Ed would establish a little income stream.

Not bad, he thought.

The truth was, he wouldn't mind seeing Eileen again.

Ed didn't spook easily.

He wasn't worried about her boyfriend. He rubbed the knuckles of his right hand.

The bigger they come, the harder they fall.

That was one of his sayings.

Maybe it wouldn't be such a good idea to work at her club, but Ed definitely wouldn't mind cultivating Eileen.

* * *

Ed heard the latch of the gate open, and a red haired woman wearing a caftan came into the pool area.

She settled into a chaise on the other side of the pool and pulled a hardcover book from her bag.

Ed, who wore a dark pair of sunglasses, tried to read the title of the book.

The woman was engrossed.

Ed got up and casually dipped into the hot tub.

Closer.

The caftan didn't do the woman justice. It didn't do a thing to set off the thick red waves of the woman's hair.

She must have had on fifteen or twenty silver bracelets and she pored over the hardback with intensity. According to the blurb on the back, the book was '*a powerful feminist's call to arms... a manifesto for the coming century.*'

The woman had pale skin with light freckles. A slash of red lipstick.

She studiously avoided any eye contact with Ed.

Ed smiled at the woman in the caftan. She briefly looked up from her reading.

Nice face, Ed thought.

Too bad she dresses herself in a gunny sack.

"I just finished reading that," Ed said, pointing at the book, "I was terribly moved."

"It's malarkey," the woman said. She had an Australian accent. "She's a total fraud."

"That's what I meant," Ed said.

Pursing his mouth and furrowing his eyebrow, he shook his head.

Changing gears.

"I guess I don't know when I've been so offended."

The woman laughed.

Ed felt encouraged.

He would enjoy getting to know this wannabe Germaine Greer.

On closer inspection, the caftan wasn't so bad.

It was a beaded fabric that was probably expensive.

Too bad it was so long.

All Ed could see were her arms and ankles.

Those were nice, though.

Tanned and slim.

The laugh was a good sign, Ed thought.

He wondered how far he could push his luck.

❊ ❊ ❊

"And just where have you been?"

Eileen stood over Ed's chaise.

"You practically disappeared from the planet."

Ed looked up at Eileen. He had been so busy watching the Australian woman, he hadn't noticed Eileen's arrival.

Which was really something, Ed thought.

Eileen's hot pink bikini was difficult to miss.

Nothing about Eileen was particularly subtle, Ed thought.

That was part of her appeal.

She held a half-full pitcher of what looked like Margaritas.

"I've been around," Ed said.

Might as well stay noncommittal.

"Come on," Eileen said. "Let's get in the hot tub."

She pulled Ed by the wrist. "Come on."

Ed looked at the Australian woman. She was still reading the book, but Ed thought he detected the trace of a smile.

She must be getting to the good part, Ed thought.

The part about the manifesto.

✳ ✳ ✳

"This time, he's really gone," Eileen said. "Really and truly."

Ed nodded. The cruiser-weight.

Ricky?

Ed had to admit that things were going a lot better this time than they had previously with Eileen.

Hearing that her boyfriend was out of the picture was good news.

Things were definitely on the upswing.

✳ ✳ ✳

"Oh my God," Eileen said, "It's huge…"

She pointed toward Ed.

"Come over here, Tanya. You've got to see this."

The woman in the caftan put her book down and looked at Eileen and Ed.

"Come on Tanya," Eileen said, "You've got to get a load of this rock."

"What are you talking about?" the woman said.

So the Australian woman's name was Tanya.

Ed filed the intelligence away for future reference.

"This little ringy-dingy Ed has."

Eileen had to be feeling the margaritas, Ed thought.

Ringy-dingy?

Ed had pulled out the ring a few minutes before.

He had made up an impromptu story about its origin.

Eileen bought it.

Tanya put the book down and walked to the hot tub. There was something definitely happening under that caftan, Ed thought.

Tanya glanced at the ring.

"It looks like it's supposed to be an Alexandrite," she said.

"Eddie's aunt gave it to him," Eileen said.

Frowned.

"She's at death's door."

Ed tried for a somber, yet hopeful look.

Tanya shook her head.

Eileen stepped out of the hot tub and grabbed the now empty pitcher.

"Wait right here," Eileen grabbed her empty pitcher. "I'm going for reinforcements."

"What makes you think it's not one of those whatchamacallits?" Ed said.

He was feeling the booze a little.

What the hell had Tanya called the ring?

Tanya held up the ring.

It had changed colors again.

"Because if it were real," she said, "it would be in a museum."

Ed laughed.

"It is in a museum," he said. "It's in the museum of Ed."

He reached up and took the ring back from Tanya.

Tanya rolled her eyes. "Right," she said.

"Back in a flash," Eileen said. "You two behave yourselves while I'm gone."

Ed glanced at the retreating form of Eileen.

He raised his eyebrows and held out his hand toward Tanya. "So how about it, Tanya? Think we can behave ourselves?"

Tanya moved away from Ed.

"Listen," she said. "Feel free to take the hell off any time you want to."

Ed drew back.

He held the ring in his hand and let a jet from the hot tub pulse around the gem.

Why was Tanya so hostile?

He didn't agonize over the question.

Although he had enjoyed a pleasant reverie concerning both women, Ed accepted Tanya's rebuff.

You win some, you lose some.

It was another one of his sayings.

❊ ❊ ❊

He was alone when Eileen returned.

A bird in hand, Ed thought.

He was ready to get down to business.

"So how about it," he said to Eileen. "How about we go paint the town red."

❊ ❊ ❊

Eileen prowled the bed like a lioness.

She propped her left knee up, adjusting her halter top and smoothing her short skirt while watching Ed take off his sports jacket, shirt, and shoes.

He kept his watch on.

Showing Eileen the town amounted to signing into a Jacuzzi suite at the Sheraton.

Ed had felt optimistic and had pulled out plastic

at the desk.

No chance of Ricky turning up here.

Things were already looking brighter.

He was even thinking about taking Eileen up on her offer of working at the strip joint.

"We should have music," she said, leaning forward on the king size bed. "That's rule number one. You should, like, never, ever go on without music."

Ed glanced at her. What the hell was wrong with this picture? Wasn't Eileen the exotic dancer? Shouldn't he be the one reclining on the bed, watching her take her clothes off?

What the hell, he thought.

If she wanted music, he could fiddle around and find something on the radio next to the bed.

Ed twirled the dial , moving the band from a country station, to talk radio, to a Mexican station before finally settling on a smooth easy listening selection.

It was a nice song about pina coladas.

Eileen unsnapped the back of her top and threw it onto the bed next to Ed. "There's something to keep you busy," she said.

Much better, Ed thought.

Her body looked even better than it had in the hot tub.

Eileen laughed and made a vain attempt at covering her breasts.

"Your turn now," she said.

Ed put a knee on the bed. "Shouldn't you be the

one doing the striptease?" he said. "I mean, you're the professional."

Eileen laughed. "Ed, honey, this was supposed to be my night off."

Ed unsnapped his flared slacks, and felt them drop to his ankles.

Eileen crawled over to the side of the bed and worked her way into Ed's embrace.

"Show me the ring again."

"What ring?" Ed said.

Eileen laughed.

"Ed, honey... I thought you wanted the full show."

Ed grinned. "Gimme the works," he said.

Eileen laughed. "I'll just need a second. I have to get ready." She stepped in front of him and cupped her breasts. "We're going to have some fun," she said. "Why don't you step in there?" She pointed to the bathroom. "I'll tell you when to come out."

Ed shook his head. "No way, baby," he said. "I'm staying right here."

"Start a shower," she said. "A cold one."

She giggled.

"I'll be ready in a minute."

Ed stood up. "We could take one together."

Eileen shook her head, and pushed him away. "Sounds like fun, but first I'm going to give you a surprise."

"Surprise?"

"That's what I said."

The steam in the bathroom fogged up the

mirror, and Ed used the palm of his hand to clear it. He heard Eileen shifting the station again, this time to a rock station. She blasted the volume on the radio's small speaker.

"Ready?" Ed shouted.

"Just a second," he heard Eileen say, "I'm almost there. No peeking."

Ed looked into the mirror.

"How about now?" he said.

Eileen didn't answer.

He wrapped a towel around his waist and stepped out of the bathroom. "Ready or not," he said, "here I come."

The room was empty.

His pants lay in a clump next to the bed. He grabbed them and fished out the wallet.

His money was gone.

He grabbed his coat from the back of the chair where he left it.

She had taken the ring, too.

He felt blood rush to his head when he pulled his shirt on, raced to the door and looked out over the balcony at the parking lot.

No Eileen.

A GLAMOROUS LIFE

Rosemary woke up early on Friday.

She looked out of her front window, wondering if Trinity was up yet.

Or even if he was home, for that matter. She hadn't recognized the woman who was with Trinity the night before.

What a glamorous life he led, she thought.

Naturally, Rosemary hadn't spent her evening staring at her neighbor's house. She didn't know what time that the woman left.

Although it had been dusk, Rosemary recognized that the woman was quite attractive.

Beautiful, really.

Rosemary needed to see Trinity, though. Professionally, of course. He would know what to do.

She hadn't seen Wendell. Sometimes when Wendell lost his temper he went back to the reservation. He would find a friend and take a sweat.

He'd built the one in the back yard, but according

to Wendell, it wasn't quite the same.

* * *

Trinity couldn't decide if he should make one more pot of coffee in the decrepit urn, or go to the Presidio Market. Twenty minutes before, the alarm clock had interrupted a dream where Trinity shared a piece of fry bread with Meredith outside San Xavier.

They were discussing baseball.

Fry bread and baseball.

Trinity thought about the dream while getting into the shower.

Coffee last night and fry bread in his dreams. He really knew how to show a girl a good time.

The hot needles of the shower worked against his body like a fierce massage. He let the water work over his calves and knees. He ran too far last night. He was so preoccupied with Meredith that he hadn't noticed the pain.

He grabbed three ibuprofen tablets from the medicine cabinet.

Tough decision, he thought, stepping out of the shower. Mess around with a coffee machine he should have thrown out a year ago, or go to the market.

No decision at all.

He walked into the kitchen. The coffee maker gave an agonizing groan.

"The hell with it," he said.

He yanked the coffee machine's cord from the wall socket, carried it to the garbage bin, and threw it away. The sound of glass shattering was satisfying.

Coffee at the Presidio Market would be ready.

* * *

Rosemary didn't miss Trinity leaving his house. She watched as he stopped, locked the door and walked down the sidewalk toward the Presidio Market. As a writer, Rosemary had to pay attention to detail. By now she knew Trinity's routine almost as well as her own.

Rosemary kicked off her slippers and fastened the straps on her white walking shoes.

She turned toward the bedroom. "I'm going down to the store, Wendell," she said.

Just in case he was in earshot.

She didn't expect an answer.

* * *

The blades of the fan gently turned high over head, providing a much needed breeze in the Presidio Market.

Lesley and April were both working today.

Lesley glanced up when Trinity swung the door

open.

"My God," she said, "look what the cat dragged in. I'm guessing you want some coffee?"

"How did you know?" Trinity said.

"Got it, Frank," Lesley said.

Walking over to the glass counter of the deli, Lesley's blonde hair was highlighted by the sun pouring in from the plate glass window.

"Impossible," April said. "This can't be Frank Trinity. It's way too early." She glanced at the clock on the wall behind the meat counter. "What is this, the crack of eight?"

April lately had taken up body building.

Today she wore a tight black leotard over her straight-legged jeans, emphasizing the shoulder length cut of her dark hair.

"Just catching up on things." Trinity eased himself into a chair at the table closest to the meat counter. The muscles in his legs were still stiff. He either needed to run a lot more, or a lot less. "Might as well give me a shot of espresso in it. I may need it."

Lesley rubbed Trinity's back as she placed his cup of coffee on the oilcloth tablecloth.

"Here you go, Frank," she said, "and that's about as much waiting on as you're going to have done for you today."

"You're closing early?" Trinity asked.

April looked over at Lesley. "Look who's developing a little sense of humor," she said, "emphasis on the word 'little.'"

Lesley rolled her eyes. "Oh, Frank's had that all along. What I'm wondering about is the grin on his face."

April looked at Trinity. "No kidding," she said, "did the welcome-wagon woman come to your place again?"

The last thing Trinity wanted to discuss was his visit from Meredith.

"Not hardly," Trinity said.

He sipped the cup of coffee. No doubt about it, it was much better than anything he made at home.

"What's this about the welcome wagon?" Lesley said.

Trinity stood up, holding the coffee in front of him.

"Can I put this in something to go?"

April laughed and pointed to the magazines by the checkout register.

"This month's Cosmo," she said. "Top Ten Male Fantasies. The Welcome Wagon. You didn't read it?"

"You know where the lids are," Lesley said.

❊ ❊ ❊

A shame to waste this weather, Trinity thought as he stepped out of the Presidio Market. It was cold, but a bright blue sky promised a good day.

He screwed the plastic lid on the Styrofoam coffee, thinking about his visit from Meredith O'Toole.

"Frank?"

Trinity heard Rosemary Gentry, and then saw her quickly walking toward him, making a frantic motion with her hands. He couldn't tell if she wanted him to stay, or if she had taken up power-walking.

"Rosemary?" Trinity said. "Did you need to see me?"

"Do I ever," Rosemary said. By the time she caught up with Trinity, she was slightly winded. "Do you have a minute?"

❊ ❊ ❊

"I understand," Trinity said to Rosemary.

He really did understand.

He wasn't surprised at Wendell's reaction, either.

Rosemary genuinely didn't have any idea about the man who had bought the painting.

"Maybe I should go to a hypno-therapist," she said.

She sounded perfectly serious.

"I don't know," Trinity said. "Let me see what I can do."

Rosemary put her hand on Trinity's arm. "You don't know how grateful I am."

Trinity pulled his arm away gently. "Let's see what happens, first."

The thought occurred to Trinity while walking back to his house.

There had been a lot of premature gratitude going around lately.

* * *

The answering machine was flashing when Trinity got home from the Presidio Market. The cup of coffee was still hot. Trinity was glad that he had taken a large this morning.

What kind of a strange thing was Rosemary Gentry telling him about?

She hadn't said anything about paying him. Probably a good thing. Where do you start with something like the painting?

Trinity supposed that he would go ahead and talk to some of the galleries in town. Let them know about the painting.

Chances were good that the painting would never be recovered.

Wendell, Trinity thought.

He probably doesn't consider himself a thief.

Doing it to help Tom...

Some help.

EL ENCANTO

The message was from Meredith.

"Call me," she said. "Page is ready to talk to you."

No explanation was needed. Trinity quickly dialed her number.

"I forgot to ask you where you live," he said.

Meredith gave him an address in El Encanto.

Trinity exhaled.

A very nice address.

"Another thing I didn't ask..."

Might as well take care of some unfinished business while he was on the phone.

There were a hundred things to ask.

"What's that, Frank?"

"It's all right, Meredith," Trinity said. It wasn't the time to ask Meredith about her life.

"I'll be over there as quickly as I can make it."

＊ ＊ ＊

"She's gone back to sleep, Frank. Do you want me to wake her up?"

Trinity shook his head. "Bad idea. From what you've told me, she's going to be a wreck."

"This isn't the first time," Meredith said, closing her eyes. "I should be used to it by now."

"Should you?"

"I should," Meredith said. She looked Trinity in the eyes. "It's my job."

"You might want to get into another line of work," Trinity said.

* * *

Meredith made coffee.

It was almost as good as the Presidio Market's.

"Good coffee," he said. "You must be back there putting eggshells in it, or something."

She laughed.

He was glad that she still could.

Her eyes were red-rimmed.

"No," she said. "Nothing like that. I just make it as is. I buy it at that little store near where you live."

Trinity looked up quickly.

"The Presidio Market," she said. "Do you ever go there?"

"Occasionally," he said.

* * *

"Do you ever pick up vibes, Frank?"

Trinity nodded his head. "They're my stock and

trade."

"Oh, I forgot," Meredith said. "You're probably the most intuitive person I know."

"Flattery," Trinity said.

"I mean it," Meredith said. "You've always been that way, even when we first met."

It was the first time that Meredith had referred to their shared past.

Trinity leaned forward. "I need to ask. Are you still married?"

Meredith formed a circle with her lips. "And just how long has that been on your mind?"

"Just while we've been sitting here," Trinity said. "Okay, that's not exactly the truth."

It was a bald-faced lie.

Trinity had been wondering about it since he first saw her standing on his porch.

Wanting to ask.

Not wanting to ask.

A smile worked itself from the corners of Meredith's lips.

"Typical Frank Trinity. Always the first person to express himself."

She fingered the hem of her skirt.

"I don't know why I didn't mention it. I suppose I'm a little embarrassed. Rob found a new friend a couple of years ago. They're happy up in Phoenix somewhere. The divorce was fairly amicable under the circumstances."

"You should have called me," Trinity said. "I could have dug up some dirt."

Meredith shook her head.

"No need for it, but thanks. I've never been better."

"You've never looked better," Trinity said.

It was true. His memory of the younger Meredith contained only a hint of her present beauty.

"Now who's doing the flattering?"

"I can't help it," Trinity said. "I'm sworn to tell the truth."

"A likely story," Meredith said.

She moved closer to Trinity.

* * *

Page walked into the living room wearing a flannel bathrobe.

Trinity stood up.

"Page?" Meredith said. "Honey, you remember my friend Frank Trinity? He's the one I said would be able to help us.

Page sat down.

She looked tired and very sick.

It might be a while before she could talk.

Trinity gestured to Meredith to get her attention.

He held his index finger against his lips.

* * *

"And that was the last you saw of the ring," Trinity said. "It wasn't there when you got back."

"I looked for it under the frog," Page said.

She put the coffee down on the table in front of her.

"It wasn't there. Then I woke up, and I had to get out."

"That's when she called me," Meredith said.

Trinity nodded. "What was the name of the woman?"

"Margo Powers," Page said. "She runs a place called Presidio Antiques."

Trinity raised his eyebrows.

Meredith looked at Trinity. "She's probably there right now."

"I know the place," Trinity said. "It's down the street from me."

Page looked miserable.

"And you're sure that your mother-in-law doesn't suspect anything?"

Page shook her head.

"She thinks it's lost."

Meredith took this as good news. "If Frank can find it, you can just put it back... can't she?"

She looked at Trinity for approval.

Trinity shook his head.

"First things first," he said. "Let's see if we can get the ring back. Then Page can decide."

✳ ✳ ✳

"I'm sorry, Frank." Margo shook her head. "It couldn't have been Jeremy."

"Let's talk about that," Trinity said. "Page said she spoke to him at your house. He was the one who told her to leave the ring. He said that you weren't there."

Margo felt trapped. She felt the walls caving in.

What could she tell him?

Sorry Frank. My husband was comatose all evening... In fact, I briefly considered suffocating him.

No, Margo thought.

That wouldn't do at all.

"It wasn't Jeremy. He wasn't feeling well. I doubt he got out of bed the whole night."

"Could I speak to him?"

Margo raised her eyes. "If he were here, of course."

"You don't know when he'll be back?"

"No idea," she said.

✳ ✳ ✳

Margo stood in the doorway after Trinity left, turning his card over in her hands. She didn't know where Jeremy had gone, let alone when he would get back.

Still, she felt guilty. What had happened to Page's ring? Could Jeremy have become coherent enough to talk to Page?

It wasn't possible.

Margo knew Jeremy.

Once he had passed out, an earthquake wouldn't awaken him.

How much was the ring worth?

It was pointless to blame Page.

Trinity had told Margo about Page. That came as a surprise. She wouldn't have suspected Page had problems.

There was only one possibility.

Whoever Matthew Fenton sent had to be the person Page talked to.

Fenton might be able to help Margo get the ring back to Page.

AT THE
SHERATON POOL

Never in his life had Ed felt quite so screwed over.

The treatment he had gotten from the department was nothing compared to this.

You stupid shit, he asked himself, when are you ever going to learn?

He sat by the Sheraton pool, waiting for the waitress to bring him his third gin and tonic. He pulled a Benson and Hedges from his pack and lighted it.

The sun blazed overhead, making it a perfect Tucson winter day, but Ed was miserable as hell.

It would have been pointless to try and follow Eileen. By the time that he had gotten his clothes on, she would have been long gone.

He had been taken again. The feeling was becoming familiar, and Ed didn't like it.

He stared at the end of his cigarette. Moisture from his fingers made the paper nearly opaque where he held it.

One screw-job after another.

The girl arrived with the gin and tonic. Her khaki shorts set off her long legs, but Ed couldn't have cared any less.

She put the drink down on the table next to Ed.

"Are you still putting this on the room?" she said.

"Exactly," Ed said, "I'll need a pen."

He was losing his job with the department. If he was really lucky, no charges would be filed.

He would probably never work again.

Trying to help his mother, he'd done nothing except rob a harmless guy of what could be costume jewelry.

It was worse than that though, Ed realized.

It didn't even matter what the ring's value was.

He was a criminal.

Things were going downhill fast.

Eileen turned out to be a thief. She'd taken his cash along with the ring.

That hurt.

Who could say if the ring was worth anything? Ed didn't know, and didn't particularly care.

What made it double-ugly was that he had even thought about giving the ring to Eileen as a Christmas present.

Well, he was a chump.

He could see that now.

No doubt about it, he was an idiot.

He stubbed the cigarette out on the pool deck and flipped the butt into the blue water.

There isn't an honest person left in the world.

What the hell was left to him?

The gin and tonic went down smoothly. A summer drink in the middle of winter. Ed looked around. There was nobody else in the whole pool area. Who the hell cared what kind of drink he had?

He looked at the palm tree overhead. A rustling of birds. They had made their nest in the overgrown fronds.

What had he been thinking of the last few days? All of his actions had been selfish.

He should go check on his mother.

Gladys would be alone.

It wasn't right for him to let his mother spend Christmas by herself.

He still hadn't maxed out his credit card. It wouldn't hurt to buy a present for Gladys. What was this? He couldn't remember if it was Christmas Eve or the day before.

Gladys always liked it when he showed up with one of those gussied up packages of lotion from Levy's.

Ed got up from the chaise.

Left the remainder of the drink on the poolside table.

He needed to see his mother.

RED RIDING HOOD

Margo stood outside Trinity's front door, pulling her cape around her.

Trinity smiled at her.

"You're looking for me?"

Margo nodded. "I haven't been waiting that long."

"Come in," he said.

"I have something else to tell you," she said.

It didn't surprise Trinity. He held the door open for her.

* * *

Margo accepted Trinity's offer of a cup of coffee.

Her red cape contrasted with her dark hair and fair skin.

Just like Red Riding Hood, Trinity thought.

"Don't worry," Trinity said. "I know Fenton. I can talk to him."

Margo looked relieved.

"Why did you call Fenton?"

Margo put the cup down. She looked at Trinity. "I panicked. I didn't know what to do. I assumed Jeremy stole it from him."

Trinity looked quizzically at her.

"I know it sounds terrible. But Jeremy was so excited by the display at the gallery. And sometimes I think that I don't even know him anymore."

"It's all right," Trinity said. He was glad that she didn't seem to be on the verge of tears.

He still hadn't bought any tissues.

* * *

Trinity had never been to Fenton's house.

The old man shook his hand and showed him in.

Fenton didn't hesitate about the painting. "I have it," he said. "It's safe."

"Your guy took a ring, too."

Fenton closed his eyes and shook his head. He took the black cigar from his mouth and examined the end. "It's delicate. But I can probably get that back, too."

Trinity nodded. "That would be kind."

Fenton put the cigar in an ashtray next to his chair.

"Mind describing this ring?"

Trinity thought twice.

"It may only be coincidence, but I think there's a connection between the ring and the painting."

Fenton squinted at Trinity. "You don't *really* believe in coincidence, do you?

* * *

"I'm fascinated," Fenton said. "Tell me again how Jeremy ended up with the painting."

"I can't give you names, of course."

Fenton impatiently waved his cigar. "I don't need them. I'm more curious than anything else."

Fenton's eyes widened when Trinity told him about Wendell taking the painting from Tom for appraisal.

"I got to tell you, Trinity. That surprises me. It really does."

Trinity had no idea what Fenton was getting at.

"I wouldn't expect you to understand," Fenton said quickly. "It goes back a few years."

He turned to Trinity.

"What do you know about Maxwell Day?"

OPEN SESAME

Fortunately, Noel was home.

Trinity rapped on the front door, and Noel opened it.

Trinity had seen Noel getting in and out of his Volvo.

Nondescript.

Trinity hadn't paid any attention to him.

According to Fenton, that was Noel's stock in trade.

"People don't notice him," Fenton had said. "He can go practically anywhere. It's kept him out of a lot of trouble over the years."

"Your name's Noel?"

Trinity watched the man's reaction carefully.

Noel let Trinity into the house.

Mentioning Fenton was the password.

Open sesame.

Noel didn't deny taking the painting.

"It was a job for Fenton," he said. "I needed money."

"What other kinds of jobs have you done for him?"

Noel shrugged. "Paintings mostly. Etchings. A

few other small pieces."

Trinity looked around the walls. Paintings hung everywhere.

"You're pretty talented, aren't you?"

Noel raised his eyes. "I try."

Trinity moved closer to one of the paintings.

"How long does it take to do one of these?"

"You might as well take a look," Noel said.

He led Trinity into the back room.

Two easels were set up next to one another.

The painting on the right was the cavalry officer and Indian. The Indian passed a pipe to the officer.

On the other easel lay a nearly completed reproduction of the original.

Trinity was reminded of the process that the old masters had used with their apprentices.

When the painting was complete, Trinity had no doubt that it would be indistinguishable from the original.

"What about the materials?"

Noel's eye's glimmered. "What do you mean?"

Trinity picked up a tube of paint. "How do you get the same colors?"

Noel smiled. "That's where art comes into it."

Trinity pointed at the easel.

"So how long will it take you to finish this?"

Noel picked up a brush. "How long will it take for the paint to dry?"

❊ ❊ ❊

Noel didn't deny taking the ring.

He held up his right hand, examining a smudge of paint across the palm.

"That was a mistake," he said. "I should have listened to Fenton."

"You can make it up," Trinity said. "Give me the ring and I'll make sure that it gets to its owner."

Noel looked toward the floor.

"I can't," he said.

SANTA CLAUS

Trinity found a parking spot for the Bronco near the Wig-O-Rama on Congress and walked the few blocks to the probation office.

No use in bothering Gladys. Ed's supervisor would know his whereabouts.

"Are you checking in?" the receptionist said. She slid a clipboard toward him.

Her demeanor expressed disapproval.

Late afternoon on a Friday with Christmas in two days...

Trinity scuffed the heel of his boot on the linoleum floor.

"I need to talk to Larry Cano," he said.

"Can I tell him who you are?"

Trinity slid his business card through the slot beneath the window. "My name is Trinity. Tell him I have some questions about Ed Carney."

"All right," the woman said. "I'll see if he's still here."

※ ※ ※

Trinity was half asleep when Larry Cano came out.

"Come on back to my office," Cano said, leading Trinity past the receptionist.

"You're asking about Ed Carney?" Cano shuffled papers on his desk.

"I've got some information for him." Trinity said. "Is his office here? I could leave a message."

"He's on leave," Cano said. "Hell, it's public record. Carney's been on disciplinary leave pending a hearing. As a matter of fact, I need to get in touch with him too. When you catch up with him, tell him to give me a call... After Christmas."

"What's the suspension for?" Trinity asked.

Cano gave a quick, dismissive gesture. "Sexual harassment."

Trinity knit his brows.

"I know, I know..." Cano said. "He's lucky. The bigwigs decided to let him off with a slap on the hand. He's lucky he isn't getting the axe. He's lucky he got Joe Sawyer on his case. The son-of-bitch threatened a counter-suit on Carney's behalf."

Trinity tried to process what seemed like conflicting information.

Cano looked disgusted. "Total bullshit, if you want my opinion. But who needs this kind of mess?"

Trinity shrugged.

"So you're saying he isn't going to get fired."

Cano nodded. "His biggest problem will be dealing with his colleagues. After something like this there's bound to be some hard feelings. But hell, it's a big department." Cano held his hands apart. "One big happy family... Everybody just gets re-assigned."

Trinity thanked Cano.

Cano grinned. "That's what I'm here for."

He paused.

"You see him, make sure you tell him he's an extra lucky son-of-a-bitch."

Trinity gave Cano a look.

"What's the extra part?"

Cano glanced around so as not to be overheard.

"I know Sawyer's secretary." Cano shook his head. "She told me he has some kind of problem."

He held his index finger next to his nose and sniffed.

Meaningfully.

"My friend says Sawyer got confused and did the whole damn thing without a retainer. That son-of-bitch Carney hadn't even paid him a dime."

Cano shook his head in disbelief.

"Makes you believe in Santa Claus."

❉ ❉ ❉

Might as well head home, Trinity thought.

He would have to get Ed's address from Gladys.

No need for that.

Pulling the Bronco in front of his house, Trinity saw Ed's gold Trans-Am parked in front of Gladys's.

❋ ❋ ❋

Ed was slumped in a chair in Gladys's living room.

Gladys let Trinity in and then excused herself.

She said something about putting up last minute lights.

Trinity suspected the excuse was made up.

The luminarias leading up the walkway in front of Gladys's house had been lit for the last few nights.

Trinity wondered if that was enough to make Wendell happy.

Probably not.

❋ ❋ ❋

Ed couldn't believe what Trinity told him.

"No way," he said. "They been after me for years. This was the excuse they were looking for."

Ed looked over his shoulder to make sure that his mother wasn't within earshot.

"What I did was nothing that a hundred other guys have done."

This was not the time to go into a discussion of modern life with Ed.

"Time's are changing," Trinity said.

Ed looked at Trinity.

"So you say…"

"It's true." Trinity said.

Ed looked away.

"So the ring…" Trinity started.

"The girl's name is Eileen. She lives at the same apartments as me." Ed rubbed his chin. "I imagine she won't be there too much longer."

"Who knows?" Trinity said.

Ed hesitated. "I wouldn't go to her apartment. She's got a boyfriend."

Trinity nodded.

"And I gave you the name of the place she works. It's right next to the Crawl-Back-Inn. You know, the place she thought I could get a job?"

"Got it," Trinity said.

"I thought she was a real nice girl," Ed said.

"You never know," Trinity said, "maybe she is."

"Isn't that the truth, brother."

Gladys stood in the doorway of the living room.

It should have been a touching reunion, Trinity thought.

"You boys need to see this," Gladys was excited. "I can't say that I've ever seen the like."

She led them out the door and up the street.

"You've got to see this," Gladys said.

*　*　*

In front of Margo's shop, a small crowd gathered, looking at the front window.

Botticelli?

Michelangelo?

Trinity knew he was looking at the work of an old master.

Or the work of an expert forger.

The Madonna and Child belonged in a museum.

In front of the store, chalk images of cherubim covered the sidewalk and led down the street.

Trinity stared at the work.

It was awe-inspiring.

Gladys was astounded as well.

She stood in front of her house, clutching her hands in front of her thin chest.

"I can't believe it," she said. "I have never seen the like."

Ed turned to Trinity.

The painting on the antique store window didn't seem to impress him.

"So, Trinity..." Ed said.

A look of bewilderment in his eyes.

"I guess you're saying I can go back to work?"

❄ ❄ ❄

Trinity pounded on Fenton's door, and waited for the old man to let him in.

The winter chill had given Fenton a chest cold and a wracking cough.

"Have Noel get the ring," Fenton said, sipping a

cup of tea, "he's a pro."

Fenton's suggestion was good.

"You think he'll do it?" Trinity asked.

"Give him directions and he'll get the job done." Fenton coughed, and touched his red nose with his handkerchief.

* * *

The chalk drawings covered all the sidewalks in the neighborhood. They led to Noel's door. Trinity knocked.

* * *

"Fenton told me that you could do the job," Trinity said.

Noel stood in the doorway, hands at his side, dust from the colored chalk still marking the front of his jeans.

Noel nodded.

"I can do it."

It was a long speech for Noel.

Having Noel retrieve the ring was poetic.

It closed a circle.

Trinity wanted to get things wrapped up.

Tomorrow would be Christmas Eve.

He didn't want to wake up on Christmas morning with unfinished business.

✽ ✽ ✽

Noel sat in the rear booth of Eileen's club.

As usual, he was unnoticed.

The place was decorated for Christmas.

The woman on the stage wore red, but not very much.

This wasn't Eileen.

Trinity had given him a good description of the woman. He needed to see her, and then he would get the job done.

The next dancer had to be Eileen.

Even if Noel hadn't recognize her from Trinity's description, he would have recognized the Alexandrite, winking from Eileen's navel.

✽ ✽ ✽

Seeing the roll of bills Noel flashed, Eileen was interested.

Cute and rich.

Funny she hadn't noticed him.

Yes, she told him, she would be very interested in getting to know him better.

He's a little different, Eileen thought.

Nice, though.

She liked his little routine with the coins.

Sitting on the edge of the bed at the Sheraton, he

made them appear and disappear into thin air.

She laughed and clapped her hands when he pulled the scarf from her brassiere. The silk didn't seem to have an end.

"Maybe I could be your assistant," she said.

"Maybe," he said.

He wasn't grabby, and he wasn't in any hurry.

Quiet.

Eileen didn't hesitate when he motioned for her to take off the ring and put it in the center of the red silk handkerchief.

The ring came off easily.

He held it up to the light and pursed his lips together appreciatively.

He folded the handkerchief several times and lifted his index finger in the air.

The handkerchief vanished.

"Hold on," he said.

She waited while he went into the bathroom.

Turned on the radio next to the bed and twirled the dial, looking for some good music.

"You still in there?" she called toward the bathroom.

That was a joke, she thought.

There was no way out of the bathroom.

He was just taking forever.

It took another ten minutes or so before she went and checked on him.

Gone.

THE PANTOMIME

Fourth Avenue was empty.

Saturday.

The morning of Christmas Eve.

How many other people in town hadn't even started their Christmas shopping?

The man in the velvet jacket surprised Trinity.

Without a word, the man pulled a jewelry box from his jacket pocket.

How did I manage not to recognize him? Trinity wondered.

The chalk paintings should have tipped Trinity off.

"You're a talented man," Trinity said to Noel.

Noel silently opened the box. His eyes widened and he leaped back in a pantomime of surprise.

Trinity leaned forward and reached for the ring.

Noel waved his hands in front of Trinity.

"How did you manage this?" Trinity said.

While in whiteface, apparently, Noel wouldn't speak.

Noel shrugged his shoulders.

Trinity knew not to ask again.

"I won't be reading about this in the newspaper,

will I?"

Noel was surprisingly articulate as a mime. His mouth and eyes stretched in replies that seemed far more germane than anything he could ever have uttered.

Noel's expressions made it clear that Trinity had nothing to fear about the way that the ring had been obtained.

Noel held out the palms of his hands toward Trinity and waggled them back and forth.

Nothing to worry about.

Trinity took the ring from Noel, and watched as he took a handkerchief from his pocket and dabbed at the corner of his eye. The handkerchief was a bright red, and as Noel pulled it out, it turned blue and then a paisley green. Noel grinned, and stuffed the handkerchief into the pocket of the velvet coat.

When he pulled his hand back out, he held a black derby hat.

He dusted the derby lightly, nodding once toward Trinity before he walked away.

❋ ❋ ❋

"What can I say, Frank?"

Meredith held the ring in the palm of her hand.

She stood in the living room of her El Encanto home.

Truly elegant, Trinity thought.

Nobody would have to strong-arm Meredith's

neighbors to display luminarias.

She stood close enough that he could practically feel the warmth of her skin.

"It's nothing, Meredith."

Meredith extended her hands.

"You always were sentimental, Frank."

Trinity pointed at the ring.

"Careful, you don't want to drop it."

He turned toward the door. "By the way," he said, "how is Page planning to get it back to Tallie?"

"We discussed that," Meredith said. "I told Page that she could just leave it at Tallie's house. Some place where the old girl can't miss it."

Trinity nodded.

"Page doesn't want to do that, though." Meredith was slightly puzzled. "She said that she would have to face Tallie eventually. She's bound and determined to give her the full story."

Meredith stopped and looked at Trinity.

"Go on," he said.

"I mean, do you think that's wise? You've seen how fragile she is. You know the odd part is that she was sober when she took the thing. Strange, isn't it?"

Trinity shrugged.

"I've heard of stranger things. The important part is that she gives it back."

"But going directly to Tallie?"

Trinity nodded.

"It's probably the best thing that she can do."

He put his hand on the door.

Meredith touched his arm. "You don't have to leave, you know. I could make dinner."

* * *

"Honest to God, Noel, I think you did great."

Fenton stood in his bathrobe. His cough was a little better. With any luck, he would live.

The painting was perfect. Fenton looked at it from every angle. He looked back and forth from the original to Noel's reproduction.

"You sure you aren't Max Day's kid?" Fenton asked.

He laughed.

Noel shook his head. "My parents are dead."

Fenton shot Noel a look. "So is Max, my friend. So is Max."

He took out his money clip and started peeling off bills. The money he gave Noel earlier was small potatoes. This was the real payoff.

"What are you going to do with all this loot?" Fenton asked.

"I'm not sure," Noel said.

Fenton laughed. It was a lot of money. More than his friend here was likely to see for a while. "Tell you what, I might have another job for you... If you're interested."

Noel looked quizzically at Fenton. "What kind of job?"

That was what Fenton liked about Noel. Even on Christmas Eve, the kid was willing to talk about a new opportunity.

It gave him faith in the younger generation.

"Have you spent much time in Mexico?"

Noel shook his head.

Fenton laughed again. A rattling laugh that turned into a cough.

"You're missing out then. Come see me after the new year," he said. "I got something in mind that might interest you."

CHRISTMAS EVE

Tom looked as if he had just awakened. He opened the door for Trinity.

"Glad you're back," Trinity said.

"A surprise and pleasure seeing you," the older man said. "On Christmas Eve, no less."

He motioned Trinity to come in.

"Are you decking the halls?" he said.

Trinity laughed.

"You wouldn't want to hear that, Tom... Trust me."

"You know I trust you implicitly," Tom said. "Come in though. It's cold out there. What, you want me to beat you again in chess?"

Trinity shook his head.

"Not tonight, Tom. I need to preserve some self-esteem."

"What's that then?" Tom said, pointing at the wrapped package Trinity held. "It must be a present for me. How nice."

"Open it carefully," Trinity said. "It's fragile."

❊ ❊ ❊

Tom ran his hand over the edge of the frame, looking carefully at the painting.

"Why did you do it?" Trinity said.

Tom looked quickly toward his neighbor.

"Do what?"

Trinity touched the frame.

"You should be proud of your work, Mr. Day."

Tom nodded.

"I see."

He was quiet for a moment.

"Can I trust you then, to keep our little secret?"

Trinity shrugged.

"It's safe as far as I'm concerned."

Trinity looked at Tom. His neighbor was preoccupied with the painting.

"I'm curious though... Why did you decide to drop out of sight?"

"I committed a crime," Tom said, laying his large hands on a ladder-backed chair in the kitchen. "It was long ago. Does anyone else know besides you?"

"Matthew Fenton, I'm sure. That's it."

Tom looked anxiously at Trinity.

"Matthew always knew. But not Tallie?"

"Not Tallie."

Tom looked relieved.

"I'm glad. I wouldn't want to hurt her more than I already have."

"She thinks you are dead?"

Tom shook his head.

"She knows I'm dead. There's a difference."

"I don't understand."

"The death certificate was from Mexico."

Tom frowned.

"It was altered, just a bit."

"The statute of limitations would have expired long ago," Trinity said.

"Not on murder," Tom said.

"Haven't you wanted to see your son?"

"My son?" Tom said. "You mean the son of the man I killed?"

Trinity's eyebrows arched.

"Who was he?"

Tom shook his head.

"He was a person I trusted. I trusted him too much."

Trinity looked at Tom's watery blue eyes. The old man was measuring him, trying to decide how much to reveal.

"Tallie never knew I found out about the two of them. As far as she knew, he disappeared. I had no idea what to do with myself."

Trinity folded his hands.

"How did Fenton enter the picture?"

"Matthew was my best friend. We grew up together,"

Tom smiled.

"To tell you the truth, I think that he was half in love with Tallie himself."

"You told Fenton what happened to the other man?"

"I did exactly that,"

Tom leaned back in his chair.

"Matthew came up with the plan. He's always been good about that."

"You would disappear?"

"Exactly. I never came back from Mexico. Matthew arranged the death certificate. Money wasn't a problem. It never has been. As long as I didn't give Fenton too many paintings, he could sell them…"

Tom smiled.

"Ask Fenton. I didn't stop painting until recently."

Trinity looked questioningly at the old man.

"My vision," Tom said. "It's gotten worse."

He took the painting from Trinity and carefully put it back on the wall, the cavalry officer still accepting the peace offering from the Indian.

"Don't get me wrong. I'm not comparing myself to Beethoven. But look at what he produced after losing his hearing."

"But if you can't see forms, or color…"

Tom shook his head.

"It doesn't matter," Tom said.

He pointed at the painting on the wall.

Was it the real thing, or Noel's copy? Trinity couldn't say.

"Fortunately," Tom said, "Matthew found me a protégé."

Trinity nodded.

Noel.

Tom turned away from the painting.

A MYSTERY

The lights reflected the street in the old neighborhood. The hundred-year-old adobes were bathed like shrines in the golden light.

The night before Christmas.

Trinity glanced over at Margo's store. The painting on her window was Noel's crowning achievement.

Trinity had seen Margo earlier in the day.

The painting had brought her luck. People had come from all over the city to see the art.

Many stayed to shop.

Her sales were good.

She couldn't remember a better day at the store.

Trinity had seen Rosemary, also. Wendell had begrudgingly accepted her story about the painting, and seemed relieved Trinity had volunteered to return the painting to Tom.

There were lights in the windows of Gladys's house. Ed had decided to be a good son.

Trinity wondered how long that would last. He had doubts about Ed.

There were no lights in Noel's window.

The only illumination was reflection from the

luminarias.

Gladys's renter was out for the evening.

Noel Brisbane...

Trinity shook his head.

＊ ＊ ＊

Trinity took one last look at the street before going into his house.

He still wondered which painting was the original.

One painting had been returned to Tom, but Fenton kept the other.

Would Fenton ever tell him which painting was the original?

Trinity could imagine Fenton's response to the question.

Fenton would insist some things were better kept as a mystery.

Thanks go to John Holliday for the excellent covers he has created for all my books.

And thank you, for reading this book.

If you enjoyed *Trinity Thinks Twice*, I hope you continue reading the rest of the Trinity series.

Please consider writing a short review on Amazon and telling your friends about the series.

As Walter Tevis wrote when making the same request: "word of mouth is an author's best friend and much appreciated."

Trevor Holliday

BOOKS BY THIS AUTHOR

Trinity Works Alone

Trinity And The Short-Timer

Trinity Springs Forward

Trinity And The Heisters

Trinity Takes Flight

Ferguson's Trip

Dim Lights Thick Smoke

Lefty And The Killers

Lefty Brings The Heat

Dim Lights Thick Smoke

Ten Shots Quick And Other Stories Of The New West

Printed in Great Britain
by Amazon